THE LOVE OF A GOOD DOG

STORIES FOR DOG LOVERS

ROBIN BRANDE

THE LOVE OF A GOOD DOG
Stories for Dog Lovers
By Robin Brande

Published by Ryer Publishing
www.ryerpublishing.com
Copyright 2025 by Robin Brande
www.robinbrande.com
All cover and story art by Surapoj Creative/Deposit Photos
Additional art by grafis media and Sinaelgicon/Canva
Ebook ISBN: 978-1-946627-83-4
Paperback ISBN: 978-1-952383-31-1

ALSO BY ROBIN BRANDE

~Winnie Parsons Mysteries~
A Mind for Mysteries
The Secret Juror
The Truth Chamber

~Science Fiction & Fantasy~
Dove Season Series
Parallelogram Series
Bradamante Saga
Heart of the Future
The Miraculous Unknown
Life with the Afterlife
Mountain Tough

~Young Adult~
Doggirl
Evolution, Me & Other
Freaks of Nature
Fat Cat
Replay
Into the Parallel
Caught in the Parallel
Seize the Parallel
Beyond the Parallel

And Many More

See the complete
list of books at

RobinBrande.com

CONTENTS

Introduction   ix

THE RESCUE   1
THE CALLING   31
BOUNDER'S LIST   55
FROM THE BONES OF AN OLD DOG   65
THE SLIP OF A RIB   131

About the Author   213

THE LOVE OF A GOOD DOG

INTRODUCTION

Two things I've loved to read since I was a little girl: dog stories and supernatural stories.

What a joy it is to combine both and write my own.

You will also find in this collection some of my other favorite topics: wilderness survival, the secret lives of veterinarians, country life, mysteries, and psychic communication with animals.

I hope you enjoy these stories as much as I loved writing them. Now let's go settle in to Nick Falls's snow-covered cabin in the high mountain wilderness. Enjoy THE RESCUE...

~Robin Brande

the Rescue

Nick opened the latch at the front of his wood-burning stove and added more tinder to the firebox. He had already shoveled out the ashes from overnight and laid a new fire first thing, so the cabin was plenty warm, but the coffee wouldn't boil unless the fire was raging hot, so he kept nursing the flames and feeding them more.

The wind had been howling since he first woke up and shaking the walls of his one-room cabin. He wasn't worried. Miners had lived here before he had, and the place was still as solid as it ever was. Snow had been steadily falling for at least the last half hour, soft and puffy flakes at first, wetter and heavier now.

Avalanche snow. Not the kind of light snow he'd been seeing the past week. Sunny days, freezing nights, thaw-freeze-thaw—put a heavy new layer on top of a weak base like that, and a slab on one of these mountains was bound to break off and go.

The wind shook the cabin again and the dog groaned contentedly in answer. She scratched at one of her ears with a long hind foot and then settled back into her nap on the old wool rug beside the stove. She looked like a half-grown bear cub with all the thick brown fur she grew even thicker in the winters. It made it so she never seemed to mind the snow no matter how long they were out in it, but as soon as they were back inside she'd lie as close as she could to any fire, and at night whenever Nick shifted on his bed she'd shift right along with him to make sure she kept on getting all of his warmth.

The water was boiling now, so he added a few scoops of Folgers and tightened the lid back on the pot. He loved that smell: strong dark coffee on a cold morning. Loved the smell of butter melting on the skillet he had heating up right next to it.

He took out yesterday's pancake batter from his half-fridge and poured a pool of it onto the steaming skillet. He glanced at the dog, listened for a moment to the soft rumble of her snore, and poured a second small pancake for her.

The wind was blowing sideways now, and heavy snow hurtled itself against the cabin windows. A gust sent the bucket of cooling ash skittering across the wooden porch, and it made enough of a clatter that Bruna briefly opened one eye.

"Just a bit," Nick told her as he flipped over both pancakes. Then true to his word he dropped the finished pancake into her metal bowl and broke it into pieces with his spatula so it would cool faster and wouldn't burn her mouth.

Snow and wind blustered over the compound. There were newer cabins across the one-track road, and there were scientists inside them huddling in their long johns and blankets and fleece this and that, maybe worrying about whether they'd get to take all their measurements today, or else grateful for a day off.

Nick was grateful for the day off, too. A day off from all the yammerers asking him questions or trying to butter him up. "Are you the famous Nick Falls?"

"I'm Nick Falls," he'd tell them. "Don't know about famous." But he knew what they meant. Knew what they wanted to know.

They all wanted to hear the story.

How did he save those people?

2

When you've been in a place for fifty years, you know it in ways the day-tourists and the summer grad students and the winter scientists couldn't possibly understand.

Know it like you start knowing your own face through its changes, every brown spot, the wrinkles, the way your eyelids sink back deeper into their sockets the older you get. Not handsome, not ugly, just an old stump of a tree out in the woods, something reliable and recognizable, a way to measure your distances across the land.

And if you know how to be quiet—really deep down quiet, not just silent, holding your words back, but quiet like the bottom of a lake—then eventually you start to hear things.

Things that aren't from you.

You start looking at maps. Tracing the contours with the tips of your fingers, feeling the paper, then when you close your eyes—and you're *quiet*—you can feel the bumps of the land underneath the map. The rough rock faces. The soft mosses down in the clefts.

You can feel the way the land slopes here, how the edge of this map slips over to the next one, and it's windy over there now, and you can smell the sticky sap of a summer pine.

Nick had a drawer filled with maps, but that was before he could hear them. Back when they were just paper, just lines, just someone's idea of how to show what the land looked like.

Nick was out in that land every day. Taking measurements. Wind speed. Temperature. Rain. Snowfall. Recording when he saw the first robin and the first buds on the aspens in the spring.

He wanted to know the place. Know it *deep*. So he started keeping records long ago, just for himself.

Never dreaming they'd be valuable some day. That they would bring the scientists here all year round, to study the changes, to study his records. To prove what they already suspected about the way the world was going.

Back in the beginning, fifty years ago when he was twenty-four, Nick was supposed to be just the summer caretaker up here. The handy-man fix-it, whatever the scientists and students who lived in the row of rustic cabins for those few months of summer might need. Mouse trapping. Roof leaks. Nursing the fussy electricity.

But as the summer yellowed into fall, and the people all left, and the days got shorter and the nights longer, and it was just Nick and the vast mountains and the woods all around him, he found he had no desire to leave anymore. For what? Go back to what? Doing construction, drinking with his crew or drinking alone most nights, trying to find love, good luck with that—there was nothing.

Whereas here. Everything.

"You don't have to pay me any extra," he told the man who had hired him for just those few months. "I'll keep the place up all winter. Look after it. Just let me live here for free."

It was lonely sometimes that first winter. That was before he got a dog. Now Bruna was the fifth one in a row of the best dogs nature ever made. It always worked out that way, whether he got them from a friend of a friend or off the back of someone's pickup, *Pups4Sale*, when he went into town for groceries once a month.

Or, like with Bruna, a reject from one of the ranches down in the valley. Someone saw her listed in the want ads, under Farm Implements. *Ranch dog, $1.* They called up Nick, knowing he'd just lost old Blue, and he skied into town the next day, all eight miles, to meet the sonofabitch who would give up such a sweet and affectionate dog because she wasn't mean enough to herd.

As soon as they were clear of town traffic and any of the people, Nick slipped the collar off her neck and Bruna had been a free girl ever since. Trotting happily at Nick's side everywhere he went, as in love with him as he was with her.

It had been Bruna who woke him up that day. Told him to pay attention.

It was still dark out. In early February, sunrise didn't reach the cabin windows until after 7:00. Nick normally got up at 5:00 anyway, just to start the coffee and go back to bed to read.

But Bruna started whining around 4:00. "It's damn cold out there," he told her. He could hear the wind beating against the walls of the cabin. But Bruna didn't want to go out, she wanted him to listen to her, to pay attention.

She paced back and forth, her nails clicking against the wood floor.

Nick clicked on the light and watched her for a minute, wondering what was wrong. He couldn't hear anything but the wind outside. But maybe Bruna heard some animal. Nick listened harder.

Bruna sat then, close to the wall, and looked up toward the map hanging there.

There were maps all over the walls now, finally out of

the drawers so that Nick could look at them every day. Contour maps of all the mountains surrounding the science station, showing the land that Nick and Bruna roamed all through the year.

Bruna kept panting, looking up at the map, whining at Nick.

"I don't know what you mean," he told her.

Bruna thumped her bushy tail against the wood floor.

She kept on like that for the next few hours. Through coffee, through pancake breakfast, through Nick checking the gauges and the thermometer and looking through the windows with the binoculars, writing down his notes on all the measurements and the observations he could make from inside the cabin. Delaying going out in the biting cold until the sun was well and truly up.

As the dark hours of the morning wore on, Bruna got more and more agitated. Pacing, nails *click click*, whining, coming over to Nick and licking his hand, sitting and thumping her tail.

He opened the door for her more than once, despite the snow blowing in. But Bruna didn't try to go out.

"I don't know what you *want*," Nick kept telling her. "What do you mean?"

Always she kept looking over toward that map.

3

Over the years, without ever trying, he'd gained a certain respect. Folks knew he was out here every day, every year, always watching and listening and learning.

A few times—more than a few—he'd fielded calls from Search and Rescue, asking for his help. Asking what he knew of the terrain this person had gone missing in. Asking if he saw any signs of rock falls or mountain lions or other hazards.

Any new avalanche slides.

Eventually they outfitted him with a radio so they could contact him in emergencies, and later a satellite phone that Nick got in the habit of carrying in his pack whenever he and Bruna went out to walk or ski the land.

He'd seen his share of dead bodies. It never got easier.

And Bruna, she hated it. She mourned about it. Whined and backed up and paced, ears flat.

"It's okay, girl," he'd tell her. "Nothing to be afraid of."

Some poor hiker or hunter or skier. It happened.

But Bruna would never be consoled. If Nick didn't move her on soon she'd start howling, letting the whole world know that something had gone very, very wrong.

Then she'd be out of sorts for days, like she took it personally. This person died, *on her land.* In her territory. She had failed somehow, ranch dog that she still was at heart. Like part of her own herd had been killed.

But it had been a while since Nick had gotten any calls from Search and Rescue, or accidentally come across a body. Over two years by then. It was a good run.

But now. Bruna was acting almost the same way. Ears back, pacing, whining.

Nick didn't want to believe it, but he was starting to.

She knew something.

She sensed something.

Maybe.

But to keep looking up at the map? What was that? Did dogs do that? Could they even understand what a map was?

It couldn't be. But Nick had seen a lot of things that surprised him in the last fifty years, and so he had learned not to be skeptical if he might learn something new instead.

Out here in this world, his own world, he found it was better to listen. To go quiet. To watch. And then if he saw or heard something he knew was true, to believe.

"We'll go out there," he told the dog. Nick started putting on all the layers he would need, five of them in total. Bruna thumped her tail, watching him. She could see she had finally gotten through.

He took his usual winter gear, permanently in his pack: headlamp, emergency kit, an extra layer of clothing, and his avalanche beacon, shovel, and probe.

If Bruna was right, if she really meant to keep looking at that one particular map, then Nick knew where they had to go.

They set off.

It was an area about five miles from the science station, accessible off a road that was closed to winter traffic except snowmobiles.

Nick and Bruna came at it from the wilderness side, where there were no roads, where no snowshoe or ski had made a print or flattened the snow all winter. It wasn't a place Nick usually went until after the snow began to thaw. There were too many hidden dips where the dog might punch through, and he had learned with his first dog how hard it was to get them out.

Now that the sun was out, the day was looking better. The snow wasn't blowing so hard anymore, but it was still damn cold.

Bruna started out ahead of him, trudging as best she could through the deep snow, but Nick told her to wait and he skied out past her so she could follow in the track he made.

After just a few strides, he got into his rhythm and he didn't have to think about what his skis were doing, he could look around.

Sunlight glinted off the pure white landscape, sparkling like jewels. Heavy pillows of snow rested on the branches of the spruce and fir. Birds sang, same in the freezing temperatures as in the warmth of summer. There were rabbit prints at the edge of the forest, leading off into the trees.

Nick knew where the streams and gullies were, beneath the cover of snow, and he steered clear of them to always keep Bruna on solid ground.

He could hear the dog panting behind him, sometimes whining. She tried to go around him a few times, maybe impatient that he was going too slow, but Nick knew of a dog who broke its leg by falling into too deep of snow, and so he kept out in front of Bruna to make the track safe.

The snow had stopped falling for now. The wind had quieted down. The morning was brilliantly sunny and cold.

But the dog was more agitated than ever.

Finally she ignored his warning and raced out ahead

of Nick. He could only pick up the pace and take longer, deeper strides, trying to keep up with her.

"Bruna!"

She barked. Not back at Nick, but ahead of her.

Up on the ridgeline, Nick could see four people. To be where they stood, they must have ridden snowmobiles part of the way, then climbed up the steepest part through the trees on their own.

Bruna barked. And kept barking. She paced, down here below at the base of the long, steep slope, so far from the people on top, Nick could barely see anything of them except their brightly-colored clothes.

The first skier took off.

The other three followed.

Bruna howled. Howled like she did when they came across dead bodies.

Nick felt a tingle all along his arms.

Something told him, but he was slow to believe it.

Take out the phone. Call them. Call them now.

Time was the only thing that mattered, in situations like this.

If this really was a situation.

Bruna laid back her head and howled again.

The mountain began to slip.

Nick fumbled with the clip on his pack. He finally released it from around his waist. He couldn't take his eyes off the mountain, off the snow, the way the slab was breaking off now, the way the whole mountainside was sliding—

But he had to find the satellite phone. Had to call. Had to get them coming, *now*. He was only one man. He needed a whole team. There were four people about to be buried.

"Bruna, NO!" She was running toward the path of the slide, in danger of being swept up in it just like the skiers. "BRUNA! COME!"

The dog howled and barked and ran a few more steps forward, but then she came back, thank God she came back, and Nick clutched a handful of her thick fur on the back of her neck, steadying himself, steadying her.

"Girl, you have to *wait*. I'm calling. Just wai—" Nick's voice hitched at the end, because Bruna looked up him then, her deep brown eyes so sad and bewildered, how could this happen? They were too slow! Too late! How could they let this happen?

"N-Nick Falls," he said when the dispatcher answered. He gave her his location. "Four skiers. All caught in an avalanche. All of them. Buried."

"We'll get there as soon as we can," she told him.

Too slow. Too late.

Time was all that mattered. In an avalanche, even if the massive force of it slamming into their bodies didn't kill them right away, snow would have filled their noses and mouths, cutting off any way to breathe.

Nick turned on his beacon to receiver mode.

But even if he was still young, even if he could still climb that mountainside, and even if his beacon picked up signals from four transmitters he assumed the skiers had on them—it would take too long. They would be buried too long. This wasn't going to work. Those people were dead.

But Bruna didn't know that. She was already racing up the slope, skidding, sliding, getting her feet solid again and running on.

"Bruna!"

She wouldn't listen.

There was no time. No time to do it the right way. To wait for help. To do what Nick had been taught to do.

Bruna had already stopped midway up the slope and was digging now, frantically digging.

Nick tried to cry out to her, but the sound clogged in his throat.

He cursed and started after her. The slope was solid enough. If this was it, if this was his day, if he died doing this, at least he died with his dog.

The skis were no good. He couldn't climb fast enough with them on. So he unclipped them and continued in just his boots.

Right about then, a strange thing started happening with his eyes.

A kind of white blindness, sunlight reflecting off the

snow, burning his eyes in a flash of pure white, making him see what he needed to see.

The snow was gone, for a flash of a moment.

He could see the four bodies, exactly where they landed.

The lowest one, the first skier who triggered the slide —that one was dead.

But the other three. There might still be a chance.

Bruna was right above one of them, continuing to frantically dig.

That one could live. But only if Nick got there in time.

From where he was, still climbing, it would take him minutes more to reach just that first body. The other two were further up. Maybe still alive right now, but for how much longer? There wasn't time to get to all of them and shovel them out enough to breathe.

He couldn't just uncover their faces. The snow was a vise squeezing their hearts and lungs. Digging out torsos took time. It took lots of shovels. Not just his own. It would be like trying to save the Titanic by bailing with a spoon.

Then that flash again. See the four bodies. *I see them. So what? What am I supposed to do? Help me!*

A thin line, tracing the slide path, noting the location of each skier beneath the snow.

Like a map.

Like an illuminated, living map.

Bruna was still digging. Digging so hard, so desperately, believing she could do it. She could save the person beneath.

Nick's breath caught in his lungs.

Goddammit, that dog. Nick knew, but he was afraid to believe. Even an open mind has its limits.

But if that goddamn dog knew something he didn't, what choice did he have but to go along?

None of this was natural. Starting with the dog waking up whining and going to the map.

Knowing something was going to happen a few hours later. Knowing with a certainty that Nick didn't have to understand before he believed.

He saw it again now, more clearly, because he allowed himself to see.

The lines of the map, drawing themselves on the snow.

The line from Bruna to the person beneath her. Then to the next skier up the hill. And the next.

Like someone laying track for Nick, making it easier, the way he did earlier for his sweet and desperate dog.

What was a map but a suggestion? A way of describing what somebody saw.

What did the mapmakers know of this land? They could only see the surface.

They didn't live in it, breathe it, take it into their minds and bodies and souls.

They had other maps to go make.

But Nick was part of this land, part of this mountain-side, and his dog was part of this land, too. She knew her responsibility to save these people.

Nick had to help her in whatever way he could.

He couldn't worry about whether it would be true. He just had to try.

From where he stood, his boots braced against the slope, he raised his right arm, level with the view in front of him. Then he extended his index finger and started to trace the line he could still see illuminated on the surface.

A thin furrow started to appear. Like ski tracks digging into the snow.

Nick pressed down harder in the air. Thought it. Saw it.

He added his middle finger, to make a thicker line. Then his whole hand, scooping away the hard-packed ice crystals, then two hands, digging like Bruna.

His legs shook beneath him with the effort of holding his position, but he didn't dare move or try to climb higher.

He didn't need to. He could do what he needed from this distance, digging away at the air.

And Bruna was digging deeper because she could now, because Nick was clearing her a path.

She got down to the skier's face. Nick closed his eyes and he could see it. He used his fingers in the air to scoop out the snow in the young woman's mouth that had hardened with just a few breaths into a plug of ice.

Bruna was already racing up the hill to the next body. Digging.

I'll be there in a second! I'm coming.

Nick dug away the snow pressing on the woman's torso. He wasn't there beside her to do CPR or to give her his breath, but something else did that for him.

The young woman opened her eyes. Cried out. She was still trapped from the torso down, but by God, she was alive.

Nick raised his hands to the next location, where Bruna was already frantically digging a hole.

Step aside, girl. Let me help you.

Bruna barked and kept digging hard.

They worked together, it only took a minute, and the man beneath the snow was alive now, too.

Just one more. Bruna struggled mightily up the slope. She was tiring. Tired. Nick could feel how exhausted she was.

He made a track for her. He knew she wouldn't come back to him if he called. She had work to do and she would do it, do it until she was done.

He traced a furrow for her in the snow. Helped her reach the highest body.

Then with his hands digging again in the air—this impossible piece of magic, but there it was—Nick and

Bruna worked together, clearing the man's throat so he could breathe, lifting the heavy snow from the skier's chest, catching life before it left him and settling it back into his frame.

Nick could hear snowmobiles in the background. Help was coming. But it would still take time for the rescuers to climb to the top of the ridge, then carefully ski their way down.

Bruna had an idea and there was no keeping her from it. She half-slid, half-ran down the steep and dangerous slope to where the lowest body lay, already dead beneath the snow.

She was no less frantic. Not taking her time because she sensed the life was gone. She whined and howled and dug like a creature possessed.

Nick couldn't bear to stand by and only watch, even though he knew the dog would be inconsolable once she discovered the death underneath.

It's okay, girl. We'll get him. But let me do it. You've done enough.

The first rescuer was up on the ridge now. The others were soon there, too. They had the right equipment. They had enough people to do the job. Many shovels. It would go better from now on.

It was strange to see the living bodies still half submerged inside the snow. They might have broken bones. Internal injuries. But that wasn't for Nick to know or to try to fix.

All he cared about now was the futile desperation of his Bruna, howling and digging out the snow. Nick wasn't sure if he could still do it with the rescuers watching. Or whether he should. It was going to be too hard to explain.

But he couldn't watch Bruna fight the snow any longer. Nick raised his two hands and he helped her dig. If anyone up the hill saw what happened, he would have to accept that. Some things were too important to try to hold yourself back.

When the head was cleared, and Nick scooped the snow out of the young man's mouth, Bruna howled in her mournful way. So Nick kept going, digging the torso free. Bruna bounced and barked on the edge of the hole.

From where he stood, Nick couldn't exactly see what went on, but the top half of Bruna disappeared into the hole.

He dug out more, and her whole body fit inside it.

She was licking the young man's face. He wasn't sure how he knew, but he knew.

The face was a vivid, shocking blue. The air had long stopped moving inside the skier's lungs. It was hopeless. But Bruna wouldn't give up.

She was made to save and protect, and she did.

Farm Implement, $1.

A digger, a herder, a machine now that wouldn't stop.

And by God, if she didn't do it.

By God, if that young man didn't open his eyes.

Nick let out a shout. He pointed. He couldn't believe it himself, but he knew what he knew.

The rescuers were all there on the slope now, shovels at work, and two of them broke away to go dig out the skier Nick had known was once dead.

"Come on, girl. Bruna! Come away now. Good girl, good girl."

Nick felt drained of all energy. He could feel it in his dog, too. Bruna limped across the side of the snow path. But her tail was wagging. She knew what she had done.

Nick knelt in the snow, arms wide open to receive her. The dog continued making her slow and limping way toward him. Then she folded herself inside. "Good girl, good girl. Best girl."

Nick buried his face in her fur.

4

She was older now, made older by her efforts. She might not last as long as she otherwise would. At seven she had the slow, careful ways of a dog twice her age. Nick had to accept that. She had done her job.

If she spent her days now more in front of the fire than out on the land, Nick would do the same. He was getting older, too. Maybe older than he should feel by now, but he didn't mind that so much. He and his dog were traveling the same road.

There was a deep down tired that Nick could feel in his bones, all the way through to the marrow. Maybe he and Bruna both left something of themselves on the slide path that day. They spent what they had, and that was all right.

For whatever reason, they'd been allowed to save four

people that day. But it seemed they were meant to do it only once, and never again. Nick doubted either of them could ever summon up the energy again, even if they tried. And that was all right, too.

In the days and weeks after, here in the deep quiet of his cabin, Nick spent a lot of time going over what he saw.

He would be a fool to doubt any part of it. Even if no one else would ever believe it or could possibly explain it.

He wrote it all down in his notes. Everything that happened. For some open-minded scientist to find in Nick's papers after he was gone, to read and ponder whether what happened might somehow be true.

Like some ancient sailor logging all the mythical creatures that he saw, out in the vast mysteries of the sea. Leave it to someone in later times to name them whales and octopi and dolphins. Leave it to the scientists to call them real.

Nick and Bruna were just explorers. Out in the unknown. Walking this land and learning what secrets it held.

Sometimes Nick still placed his palm flat against a map on his wall, closed his eyes, and let himself feel it. Feel the land and the rocks beneath the paper, feel the land coming through to his skin.

It wasn't for him to understand. But it sure was his to believe.

The dog groaned contentedly beside the wood-burning stove. She shifted her weight, found a more comfortable position.

Nick reached down and scratched her behind her ear. He felt such a love for her he couldn't describe it.

A man has a connection with a dog, there's nothing else like it. It's the most precious thing in the world. But dogs never live as long as you want them to. You have to take what they give while you can.

"Good girl," he whispered. "Best girl."

She was the last dog he would ever have, the last one he ever needed. They would walk out this long, slow road together now to the end. And that was all right with him.

The Calling

1

Surgery days were always stressful.

Even just spays and neuters, even though people thought of them as routine, were still opening up a body. Owners dropped off their dogs and cats in the morning thinking they would just go grab a coffee while the deed was done, and the animal would be good to go within about an hour. Like it was factory work.

But for Drianne it was anything but routine.

Almost fifty years old now, she had been a vet for twenty years. And she still sweated every time she sliced open a living, breathing body. It was sacred work, having an animal in her hands.

It was a calling she was too afraid to heed for the first half of her twenties. For the most part because her biology teacher in high school had scoffed at the idea.

"You could never pass the classes," he told her. "Vet school is rigorous. You're failing my class and this is easy."

Those words defined her for so long. She majored in English instead. Compromised.

Gave up.

Turned her ship toward becoming a teacher. A noble calling all its own, even though it wasn't hers.

It wasn't until she was driving her grandfather to one of his final cancer treatments that someone managed to break the spell.

"You should do what you want," he rasped through his tumor-ridden throat. "Don't listen to anyone. You can do whatever you put your mind to. You're a smart girl, Drianne."

If he had said it to her a year before, at a family barbeque or Christmas brunch, she wouldn't have given it so much weight.

But he died just a few weeks later. It became a kind of directive. The last words of a dying man.

At least that's what Drianne told herself. Because if she admitted she was doing it because it was what she had wanted to do since she was six, then that high school biology teacher's words would have won. He had already kept her away from her dream all the way through college.

But Granddad, he was a serious and driven man.

If he told Drianne to do it, she'd damn well better do it.

So she started over. And the classes were hard, no question.

But she also found a kind of grace that overlaid them.

With each test she took, Drianne felt a hand guiding her own as it filled in test answer bubbles or wrote out longer explanations on the page.

The lectures were complicated. But her ears adjusted almost right away. Like there was a translator inside her head, taking scientific concepts and turning them into real dogs and cats and horses.

Drianne could picture the diseases. The injuries.

She could see her own healing hands.

She could imagine the faces of little girls and boys, so worried when they brought in their sick animals, so elated when Drianne returned them well.

She could smell the fur. See the soft and inquisitive eyes. Each class was a new experience in meeting all the animals of Drianne's imagination. Every hour brought a new set of creatures she could imagine petting and examining and helping.

The day she graduated from vet school she felt a strong grip on her right shoulder. She was standing on the stage with the other graduates, and whipped around to see who had touched her.

No one was there. Not in the flesh.

She lowered her chin so no one would see her lips move.

"Thank you, Granddad."

She had offers from practices in bigger cities, but she wanted to stay where she was.

Rural Colorado, a small college town called Greeley, near the countryside where her ancestors had been homesteaders who built their own farms and farmhouses by hand.

Eventually the generations evolved toward more suburban lives. Drianne's mother was an accountant. Her father was an engineer.

Anyone else, other than her high school biology teacher, would have looked at those genetics and assumed Drianne would be great at a science career.

But expectations could be a burden. Whether they were expectations of failure or success.

For the past twenty years Drianne had been learning to ignore expectations and instead follow her heart.

Right now her heart was breaking.

She had an old dog on the surgical table. A fourteen-year-old black Lab named Bear. A good old boy, slow and stiff, but still with life in him. Drianne had known him for many years.

The owners, a retired couple named the Baxters who had raised Bear from a puppy, said the dog still loved his slow walks, sniffing every leaf of every bush, still enjoyed his food, even though it seemed it was getting harder for him to eat.

They thought it might be because of a broken canine tooth that looked infected. They asked Drianne to take a look.

But it was worse than that. Once Drianne pried Bear's mouth open, she could see the mass inside. The size of a golf ball, growing down from the roof of his mouth.

But she had done mouth surgeries before. Hundreds.

"I can get that out," she told the Baxters with confidence. "We can at least make him more comfortable for a while. His blood work looks good. He could have another year."

But once she got him on the table this morning, she knew at most he'd have another week.

The mass had grown so much over the weekend, it was clear the malignancy was going to cut off his airway within days. That was a horrible way to go.

A sweet old dog like this deserved better. She was relieved that the Baxters saw it the same way.

"I can wake him up," Drianne said when she called them. "Give you another few days."

"If he's sleeping now," Rella Baxter said, her voice choked with tears, "let's let him sleep. We'll be there soon to say goodbye."

Drianne had a room set aside for the terminal

patients. More like a bedroom than a treatment room. Soft lighting. Candles. A comfortable couch.

One of her vet techs rolled the mobile unit that continued to pipe in anesthesia, while the other helped Drianne carry the old dog from the surgical table into the special room and onto the couch.

Drianne put a pillow under Bear's head. His tongue lolled out of his mouth, past the breathing tube, but he looked so sweet. Peaceful. His paw even twitched sometimes while he dreamed.

The Baxters arrived, crying. Drianne told them exactly what she saw when she looked inside. Dave Baxter cried softly into his fist. Rella petted her dog and kissed his face.

"He's been sleeping about twenty-two hours a day lately," Dave said.

Drianne smiled at him gently. "And now he'll get to sleep twenty-four."

When it was time, when they were ready, Drianne administered the three successive shots. Dave Baxter had left by then, he couldn't be there, but Rella stayed on until the end.

As Drianne pushed the first syringe, she spoke to the old dog, knowing he could hear.

"You were a good boy, Bear. One of the best. Now go find another body."

Rella wept quietly, touched by those final words.

But Drianne didn't say the words lightly.
She knew by now what they could do.

2

It took a few years into her practice before she began
to notice a pattern.

Puppies who leaped from their owners' arms and
came bounding toward Drianne as if they knew her.

Kittens who purred so loudly when she held them, the
owners often laughed at how unusually vocal they were.

Dogs she met on the street who rushed to her, tails
wagging like mad, desperate for Drianne to pet them.

She had always had a way with animals. But this felt
like something more.

She was at a veterinarian conference in Denver one
year when she mentioned it to one of the other attendees.

The vet, a woman named Linda who had long gray
hair and light blue eyes, gave Drianne a peculiar look.

"Let me ask you something," Linda said. "When you put an animal down, do you say anything?"

Drianne shrugged. "Sometimes. If I know them."

"What do you say?" Linda asked.

"I tell them they've been good. And that I hope they come back some day."

Linda smiled. "Do you now."

Drianne felt self-conscious. "It's just... something to say. Why, what do you do?"

"Oh, I have a whole conversation," Linda said. "But only if I like the animal. If it's a biter or screamer or scratcher, forget it."

Drianne chuckled nervously. She wasn't sure anymore that they were talking about the same thing.

"What do you tell them?" Drianne asked. "The ones that you like?"

"That they should go find another body," Linda answered. "And nine times out of ten, they do."

Drianne stared at her a moment, not quite sure if this was a joke.

"Not all of us can do it," Linda told her. "Not everybody has the connection. But if you do..." She tipped back her plastic cup and drank the last of her red wine. "You should meet a few people while you're here. You might be interested."

3

Looking around at the mostly gray-haired group, Drianne felt distinctly young and underqualified. She was only thirty-five then, in her fifth year of practice. These vets looked like they had been practicing for decades.

There were about a dozen of them standing at one side of the conference room while hundreds of other attendees milled around and mingled.

Linda introduced her. Drianne tried hard to remember everyone's names.

They were men and women from all over the country. Gary, Indiana. Paloma, California. Chicago. Santa Fe. Provo, Utah. Cincinnati. Some with big city practices, some with small rural practices like hers.

After Linda finished the introductions, she lowered her voice and leaned closer to Drianne.

"We've all got the talent," she said.

Drianne assumed it was a slight brag. Telling her that these vets were all experts at what they did.

"I'm sure," Drianne answered politely.

An older woman who looked like she might be eighty reached out her soft hand and gripped Drianne's arm. "She means the special connection. Moving the animals on."

"Encouraging them to come back," Linda said.

Drianne was only on the brink of understanding. But before she could ask anything else, the vet from Gary, Indiana broke in. Drianne had already forgotten his name. She thought of him as simply Gary.

"Did you ever read about the Siberian fox study?" he asked.

"You mean... about domestication?" she said.

"Right," Gary said. "Back in the 1950s a couple of Russian scientists captured hundreds of wild foxes, then chose only the most docile, friendly ones to breed. The ones the scientists could touch without the foxes biting. Within a few years, they had a whole generation of foxes who would lick their faces and follow them around like puppies."

"That's what we're doing," Linda told her. "Those of us who the animals can hear. Every time we have to euthanize one of our favorite dogs or cats, we tell them to find new bodies and come back."

"It's our own way of evolving the species," Gary said. "Making sure we have more of the kinds of animals we all love. Fewer of the crazy ones and the biters."

Drianne almost laughed. It was too unbelievable. But as she gazed around at the group of seasoned veterinarians, she saw that many of them were nodding, their expressions serious. The rest were listening comfortably as if all of this bizarre information were all completely known and normal.

"You said you've seen young animals who seem to know you," Linda said.

"Y-yes," Drianne said.

"Of course they remember you," the soft-handed woman in her eighties said. "You were kind to them. Animals want only the most loving vets, too."

"So... you can all do this," Drianne said, looking around at the group.

"And you," Linda told her, "I'll bet. But there aren't very many of us. I'm always on the lookout at these conferences for more." She gestured toward her silver-haired colleagues. "We're a dying breed. We need new blood. I hope you'll go home and try it, and then tell us what happens."

4

In the days following the conference, Drianne felt as though she had stepped into an alternate universe. One where vets had powers she'd never imagined.

But of course she wanted to try.

It was the most exciting thing she'd ever heard.

Euthanizing animals had always been the worst aspect of her practice. People expected her to be stoic. Detached. Unemotional.

But she often had to leave the room right away after administering the drugs, to go have a private cry behind the closed door of her office.

Helping an animal die was a sacred duty to her. She wanted it to be as easy and as loving as possible. But it was still taking a life. She would never think of that as routine.

But now. Now she had a new appreciation for her role.

And new hope that she might do something more than just ease an animal out of its suffering.

She had an opportunity to try it just a week later.

Agnes was a beautiful old gray and white Maine Coon cat belonging to one of Drianne's favorite owners. Tracy Morrow had strung out the end as long as she could.

But finally Agnes wasn't eating or drinking anymore. And when she walked, it was clear the cat was in terrible pain.

"I could wait for her to go naturally," Tracy said. "But what if the pain keeps getting worse? I can't do that to her. It's not fair."

She sat with Agnes sleeping on her lap. The cat's normally well-groomed thick fur looked ragged and matted.

Agnes continued sleeping while Drianne began to examine her.

When she lightly touched the cat's belly, Agnes's eyes flew open and she hissed.

Tracy began to cry. "Please. I can't let her hurt another night."

Drianne prepared the three shots. She knelt in front of the chair where Tracy held sweet Agnes on her lap.

"You've been a good girl," Drianne said as the needle penetrated the vein in Agnes's front leg. "Thank you for letting us know you. Now go find another body."

Tracy wept at those words. She held Agnes to her chest while Drianne administered the remaining shots.

Drianne laid her stethoscope gently against Agnes's heart.

"Look how peaceful," she whispered. "She's gone."

Drianne left the two of them alone in the room.

This time Drianne didn't feel the urge to cry.

Instead she hurried to write in the private journal she had bought, recording Agnes's name and the date and some details about her personality and her life.

Then Drianne waited. While months went by.

In the fall, she saw Tracy Morrow listed on her schedule for the day.

A new kitten. Another Maine Coon.

Drianne knew it from the moment she entered the examination room.

The kitten started meowing at her so energetically, nonstop, it made Tracy laugh out loud.

"Well!" she said. "Guess Miss Abigail has something to say!"

But it was the kitten's gorgeous green eyes, boring so intensely into Drianne's, that made her know the two of them had known each other before.

"Hello, beautiful," Drianne said, taking the kitten from Tracy's arms.

She turned away so the owner wouldn't hear. She whispered into the kitten's ear, "Welcome back."

5

Now, fifteen years later, Drianne still treated many of her former patients.

Her favorite Labradors with their sweet, goofy smiles.

A mixed-breed shelter dog who was once a Golden Retriever who saved the family's young daughter from drowning in the lake.

The Bernese Mountain Dog who was once a Dachshund who must have dreamed of being a big dog for a change.

Cats who had lived their full lives and brought joy and love every day to their owners. Now back as playful kittens with enough fresh energy to carry them through another full and joyful life.

And even though some owners vowed they could never get another dog or cat, that it was too painful to say goodbye, Drianne heard time and again about the coincidences.

"I was just walking by…"

"My neighbor's cat had kittens. As soon as I saw them, I couldn't resist…"

"This fella just jumped right into my lap! How was I gonna say no?"

Drianne sometimes had to excuse herself, pretend she needed a fresh thermometer or some other equipment, just so she could stand in the hallway outside the exam room and allow a few tears to fall.

The animals missed their owners, too. That much was clear. It wasn't just Drianne directing the show. Maybe some of them would have made their way back on their own, even if she never told them to find new bodies.

Those animals felt their own calling. To bring joy to these particular people.

Like the Siberian fox experiment in reverse. Sweet animals helping the human race evolve over time, making them happier and kinder, one person at a time.

Drianne's private journal was now several volumes long. She sent regular reports to the rest of the vets in her special group.

Many of the old ones were gone now. But Drianne and Linda had been finding and recruiting others at the annual conferences.

More vets with the special connection. The special breed who could communicate with their dying patients.

It was sacred work, Drianne told them, having an animal's life in your hands.

All the more sacred when you could welcome them back.

As sacred as being a high school biology teacher who could encourage a young woman to follow this path.

Or could almost rob her of her true calling with just a few cruel and thoughtless words.

Words carried power. Drianne never doubted it anymore.

Words from a grandfather. *"You can do whatever you put your mind to. You're a smart girl, Drianne."*

Or from the veterinarian whose job it was to offer a peaceful goodbye. Even though ending the life of a precious animal still always left a pain in her heart.

They might come back—she hoped they did—but *this* animal, *this* version... she would never see exactly this one ever again.

It was why tears still gathered in her eyes when she had to help one of her favorites go.

But now she also knew to wait. The joy would come again.

From a Persian who was now a scrawny feral cat who had to travel miles to find his human again.

From a gangly mutt someone got from the pound,

who used to be a majestic old Collie that Drianne still missed.

All of them answering the Calling in their hearts.

That calling was love. Love between animals and their humans.

It never got old. She never got tired of it. This work was what she was meant to do.

Drianne turned out the lights at her clinic.

Knowing this place would call her back in the morning.

Bounder's List

BOUNDER'S LIST

You ask how we will ever communicate with alien species.

You ask me why I have such confidence.

Let me tell you a story.

When I was a boy, our family had an Australian Shepherd. Smartest dog I've ever known. My parents used to joke that Bounder could rewire our whole house while we were gone if we didn't give him enough jobs to occupy his mind.

So my brother and I, just for fun, just as a weird project, came up with a long list of duties for Bounder to do every day while we were at school. Things like check all the doors to make sure they were closed and locked, pick up any dirty clothes any of us left on the floor—that sort of thing.

I even wrote down the list and put it up on our fridge with a magnet, low on the door where Bounder could see it. As if he could read. But I was only eleven or twelve, and I had no inhibitions about what was and wasn't possible. Those kinds of things don't seem to grab us until we're teenagers.

One day when I got home from school, Bounder was waiting for me by the door, wagging his tail in a nervous kind of way. As if he had done something bad and knew he was in trouble. You know how dogs show that. They have terrible poker faces.

But I loved the dog and always treated him like a buddy. I asked him what was wrong, and to show me. I said he wasn't in trouble, let's go figure this out.

There was a dead bird in our back laundry area. I have no idea how it got in. All the windows in our house had screens.

Bounder whined and pushed on the bird's stiff body with his nose. I think it was a sparrow. One of those common gray birds you see everywhere, so you don't pay attention.

"What happened, boy?" I asked him. Bounder whimpered and backed up. Agitated, clearly. But I could tell he wanted me to follow him.

He took me to his water bowl. Now keep in mind, Bounder was a very tidy dog. He was long past tipping over his food bowl or his water. That was for his puppy stage, and he was a full-grown adult.

But his water bowl was lying upside down. There was still a little leftover dampness on the tile floor. I righted the bowl and saw pressed into the bottom of it a small gray feather. I knew where that had come from.

And then ... I saw it all. Bounder sent it to me as one complete package, into my mind. He showed me the whole story of what had happened.

I knew I didn't imagine it, because my imagination wasn't that inventive. The information came into my mind from the dog, I have no doubt. Here is what he told me.

When all of us left for the day, my brother and I went first to catch the bus. Then my father and mother took off to work, but my father forgot something and had to come back.

In his hurry, he left the front door open while he looked for whatever he'd forgotten. And a bird flew in. I have no idea why. That wasn't normal bird behavior.

My father didn't notice it, and soon he ran out the door again and shut the bird inside our house.

Bounder had already completed the first task on his list, to check that all the doors were closed and locked, but now he had to start over again. He didn't mind, he told me in this story he passed wholly into my mind. He began his routine again, trotting from door to door to door, and that's when he discovered the little gray bird flitting itself frantically against our living room window.

It was upsetting. Bounder didn't know what to do. He was a shepherd, not a bird dog, so his instincts didn't include chasing the bird down and carrying it around in his mouth.

The bird tried other ways of getting out. Throwing himself against different windows.

At some point the bird was just exhausted. And that was when Bounder's gentle ways came into play.

He convinced the bird to come get a drink. Don't ask me how. Can dogs and birds communicate? Not with barks and tweets, but maybe telepathically, between species? I have no idea. I'll admit it frustrates me that I don't know.

However he convinced it, the bird did in fact come to Bounder's water bowl and perch on the edge of it and take little sips. I could see it in Bounder's memory ball. That's what I've come to think of it as. Then Bounder ... again, let me say what a gentle and wonderful dog he was. But he took the bird in his mouth and crunched down, and dumped the bird in the water.

And Bounder stood there for a minute or two watching the bird float. Then he hit the bowl with his paw and dumped the bird and the water on the floor.

He picked up the bird in his mouth and carried it gently into the laundry room. He laid it on the floor, just where Bounder showed me when I got home from school. And the dog was upset about it. I could feel him asking me in his memory ball, *Did I do right? Am I in trouble?* I just stood there looking at the whole situation and seeing it from Bounder's perspective, and I had no idea what to think or say.

I scratched him behind the ears. "It's okay, boy. I'll take care of it now." I got a paper towel from the kitchen and came back and picked up the dead bird and carried it outside, thinking I might bury it.

Or maybe just throw it in our outside garbage can. I stood there holding the bird while Bounder stared up at me with his mismatched eyes, one an eerie ice blue and the other a deep brown, and he looked at me like I was some hero come to save the day. Hardly.

Outside under the crab apple tree in our front yard, I found three more dead birds. All the same species as the bird in my hand. Bounder saw them, too, and whined.

I went to the garage to get my dad's shovel. I wasn't about to start picking up all the others just with my hands.

On the way to the garage I found two more dead birds. It was insane. Like a Hitchcock movie.

So what was it? What happened? Some kind of disease?

It was pesticide. Our neighbor had blanketed his lawn with it. Some of it must have drifted over to our yard and coated the apples and the tree. Maybe the birds ate the apples, or maybe the pesticide just got in through their skin. I don't really know. But the bird that got into our house was already sick, I think. And what's more, I think Bounder knew it, too.

So then you think, wow, so what was this—some kind of mercy killing?

Not exactly. At least not how Bounder told me in the memory ball he sent to my mind.

It was one of his duties, the last one on the list I had made up for him, in big handwritten letters: PROTECT OUR HOME. I was just a kid, messing around, thinking up duties for our family dog.

I'm not saying Bounder could read it—I'm not going that far. But there's no question in my mind that Bounder knew what we wanted and expected from him. He was a guard dog, after all, that breed. He evolved to come up with ingenious solutions to whatever dangers were threatening the flock.

So a bird got in and was acting strangely, and the dog knew something was wrong. He couldn't chase it around in the air, but he somehow lured it down to the ground where it would perch on his water bowl. Then you know the rest.

And that is why I can say it with such confidence: We don't have to worry about communication with another species. We don't have to understand the same language. The information will get to us anyway.

It will get to you anyway. Trust that.

So the question isn't whether we will ever communicate with aliens. The question is, are you one of the people who will be ready to hear it? Are you training your mind right now to accept the kind of information that someone else will assume isn't real?

Are you the kid who just throws out the dead bird and goes back to his boring life?

Or are you like me, and ready to hear the chatter in the stars?

From the Bones of an Old Dog

Tom Rubey knew it was probably a lie.

He wasn't stupid and he was a fair judge of character, so whenever Nathan Weaver said something Tom automatically only half listened.

Nathan knew about Tom's dog. The whole school did. How a truck ran over Rip and never even stopped to check. A rusted-out red truck, Billy Jane Culver said, left tail light busted, but she didn't see the driver, the truck was gone before she could look.

She ran out onto the street to see if poor Rip was still alive.

He lifted his golden head, whimpered, then his head dropped heavy back to the ground and Rip was dead.

Only seven. He still had at least seven more years left,

as far as Tom knew. Rip's dad Sargent lived till he was fourteen.

That was old for a big dog, the vet said at the time. Sargent had slowed down and his teeth were rotting and his back legs couldn't walk a straight line anymore, but he was still a good birder and he could give a shaky, palsy point. Labrador Retrievers aren't normally good pointers, but Sargent learned the skill on his own. Tom and his dad had good hunting with him almost all the way to the end.

Rip was already in the understudy position, bringing up the rear. He came out of Sargent's fourth stud litter, thirteen pups that time, and Tom got to pick out which one he wanted. Rip was the only one who looked Tom right in the eyes.

By the time Sargent died, Rip was in his prime. He could go all day, running up hillsides, chasing down doves across a mile of field, swimming across lakes to bring back ducks, you name it. Tom's dad said he might be an even better hunter than Sargent.

But Rip was mostly Tom's dog. He slept at the foot of Tom's bed every night, even though over time both Tom and Rip got bigger and there wasn't really room for them both. At some point during the night Tom would stretch out his legs in his sleep and Rip would jump down onto his dog bed on the floor, but both of them still started out every night together just like they did when Rip was a puppy.

And now after just seven years together, it was over.

After the red truck drove off, Billy Jane screamed out for people to help. They got Rip's body off to the side of Dutch's Frosty Stop Drive-In. One of the cooks brought out an armful of dish towels so they could cover him.

A crowd of kids gathered. But it was Billy Jane who took it upon herself to come running all the way to Tom's house to tell him Rip was dead and she saw it.

Rip's blood was still on her pale blue dress.

"I'm sorry, Tom," she said, bawling. She could barely get out the words. Finally she told him the whole story. Everything she saw.

"I don't think he suffered," Billy Jane said, but Tom could see in her eyes she wasn't being honest.

He didn't want to cry in front of her, he had always liked her, but something like this, it was hard to stay strong.

He cleared his throat instead, tried to seem like he was fine. But he had to swipe his hand across his cheeks several times.

"Thank you—" Clear his throat. "—thank you for telling me."

"Are you going to get his body?"

Tom nodded. He couldn't look Billy Jane in the eyes right then. He knew he'd start bawling too. They were both in the eighth grade. He was too old.

His dad was at work and his mom was visiting her

sister, so Tom had to find the supplies himself. He got a few green plastic lawn bags and a wheelbarrow. He just needed to get Rip home.

All the way back to Dutch's Frosty Stop, Billy Jane kept asking him if he was all right. Tom nodded every time, but he kept his head down so she wouldn't see.

He needed to cry so badly it felt like a tidal wave inside his throat.

He didn't want to look at Rip's body. He wished none of this was real.

There were still a bunch of kids hanging around Dutch's. Tom could see a kind of cruel eagerness on a few of their faces, Nathan Weaver's included, wondering if he was going to break down like a girl.

Tom tried to be like his dad. Very matter-of-fact about life and death. He was a carpenter and he'd been around a lot of job sites over the years, and men died of this and that and they just had to deal with it. Heart attack, accident on the site, truck accident on the way there. Things happened, life wasn't perfect. Tom's dad wasn't emotional about it, he understood that was the way things went.

If he was there with him now, Tom knew his father would be kind to old Rip and wouldn't be rough loading him into their car, but he also wouldn't act like it was the greatest tragedy in the world. Dogs died. When they woke up one morning and found old Sargent had died during the night, Tom's dad shook his head sadly and went out and dug a hole. He didn't cry about it, he just got on.

Tom cried, but he was much younger then. And his mother wept about it for days.

As Tom stood now next to Rip's outstretched body beneath all the towels, Billy Jane started crying again. She and a few of the other kids helped Tom cover Rip with the green plastic bags and then lift him onto the wheelbarrow.

Blood had soaked into the ground beneath where he'd been laying. A lump globbed in Tom's throat. He had to look away.

"Want help?" Randy Hudson asked him. He was one of Tom's best friends.

"Nah," Tom said as he picked up the two wooden handles of the wheelbarrow and found the balance point on the front wheel. "Thanks." He gave Randy a nod and pushed away from Dutch's Frosty Stop.

Billy Jane came with him.

She didn't talk much on the walk back. She kept watch on the plastic bags, and made sure to cover up Rip again any time they shifted.

But Tom kept catching glimpses of his dog. The yellow coat, his big goofy feet. A corner of one of his soft ears. This dog had been alive this morning. Tom knelt in front of him before school and scratched behind those ears the way he always did, and told Rip he'd see him later.

The dog hung out his tongue and wagged his thick yellow tail. And when Tom came home in the afternoons, Rip would be standing at the door waiting, tongue out, tail wagging.

Not today, though.

Tom pushed through the screen door, let it slam behind him, and expected to find Rip right there.

He knew the dog had his own life during the days. Dog friends to visit. Even a few businesses where they kept treats for Rip and some of the other regulars who stopped by.

People visiting from out of town sometimes reported them to the dog catcher. *Dangerous dogs roaming the streets!* Mr. Culver would nod very seriously, take down the report, then rip it up as soon as the stranger walked out.

Tom knew because Billy Jane was the dog catcher's daughter. She loved animals almost as much as Tom.

But something had gone wrong this time. Rip might have been on his way home to be there before Tom was back from school when the red truck with the busted tail light creamed him and kept on going.

Tom couldn't help it now. He sniffed back his runny nose and lifted his shoulder to try to wipe more tears off of his cheeks.

Billy Jane looked at him sideways and patted him on the back.

"It's terrible," she said softly. "I'm so sorry."

Tom let out a brief sound of grief and then stifled it and kept on pushing the wheelbarrow.

He had never appreciated Rip enough. A dog like that. Always looking for the fun. At Tom's side whenever it was time to go somewhere together, even if it was just up the block to visit Randy or one of the other kids. Rip trotted along with Tom as if any outing was an adventure. Then he'd lie on someone's porch while Tom played catch or threw around a football, and the minute Tom called him again he'd come running.

They fished together on Stilt's Pond in the little canoe Tom's dad helped him make. Rip would sit in the bow staring straight ahead, and whenever Tom caught a fish he held out to Rip so the dog could give it a lick.

The dog was up for anything, always eager, always playful.

Never again. Tom still couldn't believe it.

Finally they reached his house. He rolled the wheelbarrow out back and set the metal legs down on the ground. He was sweating hard now, even though for May it wasn't that hot yet. Summer would be here soon, and in Macon, Missouri that meant humidity so thick the dogs and people alike could barely stand it.

Most of the kids went to the town pool every day, but

dogs weren't allowed. Tom took Rip out to the pond and let him dip in there, always with an eye out for snapping turtles and the poisonous water moccasins that hung around the water. On chore days when he didn't have that much time, the two of them just ran through the sprinklers.

But a day like today, sunny and not too hot, it would have been fun just to throw the ball to Rip in the back yard, then sit around in the shade and split a popsicle.

"Tom?" Billy Jane asked in a quiet voice. "What are you going to do now?"

Tom looked down at the lump covered in green plastic bags.

"Guess I'll dig a grave," he said.

Billy Jane nodded. She laid her hand on Tom's arm. "Want some company?"

"No." He looked up at her, met her tearful eyes. "Thanks."

Billy Jane made a sound like a small sob, then turned around and left.

Tom moved the wheelbarrow under the porch where Rip could have some shade.

Then he went off to the shed to get a shovel.

Out between the two maple trees in the back yard there was a wooden marker Tom's dad had made for Sargent. His dad was a good carver, but Tom wanted to make Rip's marker himself.

Tom helped his dad dig Sargent's grave, although he was younger then and didn't have much muscle. He remembered how hard it was, though, and how much longer it took than he ever expected.

He knew it would take him several hours to dig the hole all by himself, but he wanted to get started before his dad came home and offered to help. If Tom's hands were blistered by then, he might accept the help. But for now he wanted to do this for Rip on his own.

Now that no one could see him, he let the tears freely flow. They mingled with his sweat and dripped off his nose down into the turned-up soil.

It was hitting him now, the finality of it all. How one stupid careless truck driver could take away Rip's life. How quickly everything could change. How uncertain everything was.

Tom shoveled the dirt near to Sargent's grave, but far enough away that he wouldn't disturb the bones. Father and son lying close to each other, maybe still hunting if dogs had souls. Tom would never suggest that to his father, but he thought it nonetheless. What kind of world was it if a dog was just here for a few years and then died, and that was all he ever did? Why even bother creating dogs? There had to be more, especially with the kind of eagerness Rip brought to life. Of course dogs had souls.

Tom hoped Rip could see him now.

After an hour of constant digging, Tom heard his mother calling to him from the house.

He watched her come out, see the wheelbarrow, and then keep hurrying to Tom.

She took him into her arms. Tom laid his head against her chest. She was crying. She must have already heard. Word could always spread so fast.

"Oh, sweetheart," she said. "I'm so, so sorry. He was—" She choked on a sob. "—such a good dog!"

By now Tom had already cried out all his tears. "I know," was all he said. Then he pulled away to keep on digging.

"I'll bring you some lemonade," his mother said.

Tom nodded, but then thought better of it. "Can I have a popsicle instead?"

She brought him a cherry-flavored one, and he sat at the edge of the hole and took a break. When he was halfway through it he broke it in half and dropped it and the stick into the grave.

It felt right. As right as it could, considering how wrong this all was.

The day felt warmer now and he didn't want Rip to start to smell.

Tom got back to work and dug harder.

2

"Lord, we thank you for Rip," his mother said during grace.

"Amen," Tom and his father both muttered.

The digging went faster once Tom's dad got home.

They wheeled Rip out to the grave and between them gently lowered him into the hole.

Tom wanted to shovel the dirt back in by himself. His dad gave him a nod of approval and went back in the house.

That night Tom put off going to bed. He sat in the living room, he sat at the stiff uncomfortable chair at the kitchen table, he sat and walked around until he knew he was tired enough to sleep.

Still, when he lay down between the sheets, the bed was too large and his legs stretched out too early. He lay awake thinking of Rip alone in the lonely hole. Close to Sargent, but not really together.

It was morbid, thinking of their two dead bodies, but it was all he could imagine as he finally fell into sleep.

The next day was Saturday, and Tom went about his chores with a kind of numb mechanical process. Mow the grass, wash the car, clean his room, weed the yard.

He talked to Rip in his mind, describing everything he was doing, telling him what a good dog he had been and how he wished they could go to the pond or down to Randy's house or over to Billy Jane's, where they never went, but now Tom wished maybe they could.

Billy Jane would have petted Rip's head and talked to him in that kind of baby talk girls used that always sounded so ridiculous, but dogs always loved it. Billy Jane was good with dogs. She'd go help her dad at the pound on Saturdays and take the dogs out of their cages and walk them. She helped put up fliers to find their owners. Tom listened to Billy Jane and her friends talk about it sometimes. She said the vet told her when she was older she could come work over there.

On Sunday Tom and his parents went to church.

Nathan Weaver's father was the pastor. Proving that just because you're a pastor's kid, that doesn't make you good. Nathan was a liar and a bully and a show-off. Maybe he thought he could get away with it because of who his father was, and it seemed to work with the grown-ups, since they never wanted to believe how bad he really was, but the kids all knew it and everyone stayed away from him. Nathan was a jerk.

He liked to brag about all the important people who came to visit them at their house. Preachers from bigger towns, missionaries who had been to Africa, even a famous gospel singer once whose car had broken down in Macon on her way to a bigger church in Kirksville.

This Sunday was no different.

"He taught me some words in Swahili," Nathan was telling some of the boys. He said a few words that sounded invented. "He just came back from the Congo. He's staying with us the next two days."

Tom looked over where Nathan was indicating, to a stooped-over very thin man who looked too old to have survived in the jungle. He was clutching a very worn-out Bible to his chest and nodding piously to one of the old ladies from the choir.

Tom could hear her say, "Bless you," as she gave his thin arm a squeeze. The thin man moved on to another group of people.

"He's taking a collection," Nathan informed his reluctant audience. "He's going all over Missouri for the next four weeks. Then he'll use the money to go back and build a school."

Sure enough, Tom saw Pastor Weaver following along

after the missionary with a collection plate that was already full of quarters and dollar bills.

"You should hear him, Tom," Nathan said, suddenly turning in his direction. "He told us the strangest story last night."

Tom hated to give Nathan Weaver even an ounce of attention, but Nathan didn't usually single any of them out. He only wanted to talk about himself. Sometimes it was if he pretended he didn't even know anyone else's name.

"He said he was witnessing to a group of natives about Jesus being resurrected. They got all excited and told him through an interpreter that they already knew."

"Knew what?" Tom asked with barely-masked hostility. He still remembered the look on Nathan's face when Tom came to carry away Rip's body. That kind of wicked satisfaction some people take in another person's disaster.

"About resurrection," Nathan said. "Their healing man had raised lots of people from the dead."

This, finally, was of interest to the crowd. A lot of heads turned in Nathan's direction. He smiled at the new popularity. He milked his story as much as he could.

"Yeah, they said he had just saved a little baby a few days before. The parents had already buried it, but the healer had them dig it up again and he brought it back to life."

A chill swept up Tom's spine.

But Nathan was a liar. He couldn't fall for this.

"How?" Randy Hudson asked. A lot of the other kids voiced the same question.

Nathan drew himself up. He was a big man now. The undisputed center of attention.

"You want to know how?" Nathan asked them.

Kids nodded.

"You really want to know?"

"Come on," Tom said angrily. This was getting ridiculous.

Nathan grinned at him. "Bet you want to do it for your dog."

"Shut up," Billy Jane said. Tom hadn't seen her come over. She was wearing a yellow dress with a bright white collar, a flowery straw hat, and white gloves like the other girls wore to church in the spring.

There was a large group of kids around now, and more and more were joining.

Nathan must have had some realization just then, because he looked around nervously for his father. Pastor Weaver was at the far end of the church, still chatting with his congregation and collecting their donations.

Nathan motioned for the crowd to draw in closer.

Normally Tom would have resisted, but this time he couldn't.

Nathan continued in a quieter voice. "He told the parents to go dig up the body of one of their ancestors."

"Ew," one of the girls said.

A few of the boys rolled their eyes.

"Then grind up the bones," Nathan said, "and put them inside a pot with a hole in the lid. You dig a hole that's big enough for the pot, and put a jar or some other kind of container in the bottom of it. Then you turn the pot upside down so the hole in the lid is right on top of the jar."

"I don't believe any of this," Randy Hudson said. "You're just making it all up."

Tom appreciated his friend for saying it.

"It's too complicated," one of the other boys said.

Nathan made a *pssh*ing sound. "You're bringing back somebody from the dead. You think that's supposed to be easy?"

That seemed to settle down the rest of the skeptics.

"So the pot is upside down in a hole," Nathan continued, "and the hole in the lid is on top of the jar. You got that?"

His listeners nodded.

"Then you put wood all around the pot. You make a big fire and you keep feeding it more wood all night."

"Like making a stew?" one of the girls asked.

"No, stupid," Nathan said. "Did I say there was any water in there? It's just the bones."

The girl blushed. Tom hated Nathan all the more for it.

"So what?" Tom said. "You're burning a bunch of bones. Probably smells bad, but they're just burnt bones."

"Shows what you know," Nathan said with the kind of arrogance Tom was used to. "The bones melt into *tar*."

Tom and Randy exchanged a look. Neither of them really knew enough to argue.

"Then the tar drips into the jar beneath the pot, understand?" Nathan said. "That tar is what you use."

Billy Jane stood protectively in front of the girl Nathan had called stupid. She held her head high, chin on the level. She wasn't going to be pushed around.

"I've never heard of any of that," she said. "Randy's right, it sounds made up."

"Why would you have heard of it?" Nathan said. "It's from the *Congo*. You've never been outside Macon."

Billy Jane frowned, but she didn't argue.

And Tom had to admit to himself, he was still listening.

"So then what?" Tom asked.

Nathan's smile was far too triumphant. He knew he had Tom dangling from his hook. Tom hated it, but he had to know.

"The healer poured the tar on the grave of their dead baby. He said whatever spell they use there. The missionary told the parents they shouldn't have done that, it might be praying to the devil, but they said the healer only ever prayed to their gods. The healer told them to come back and check the grave in the morning."

Nathan paused, looking around at his audience and relishing their suspense.

But Tom wouldn't be the one to break it.

"Well?" Billy Jane said. She crossed her arms over her chest.

Nathan imitated the sound of a crying baby.

Kids gasped. *"No."*

Nathan smiled and nodded. "Yes. Good as new."

A kind of awed silence overtook the group. Kids looked from one to another.

Billy Jane caught Tom's eye. She looked skeptical, but she shrugged.

As if to say, *It might be worth a try.*

3

Tom waited for Nathan to come out of church. Waited for him to be alone with just his folks. Even better, Pastor and Mrs. Weaver were busy talking to the missionary, so for the moment, Nathan was alone.

Tom motioned him aside. Again, that triumphant look on Nathan's face. But Tom had to ignore it.

"What words did the healer say?" he asked.

"They were in Swahili," Nathan said in that sarcastic tone that made Tom want to punch his rabbity face.

Tom took a breath and maintained his calm. "But what did they *mean*," he asked.

"I don't know," Nathan said. "Ask him." He pointed to the stooped-over missionary.

There was an ugly tilt to Nathan's lip, as if daring Tom to go get in trouble.

But if any of that story was true, Tom was willing to take the risk.

He waited until there was a break in the conversation among the grown-ups, then he quickly approached the missionary.

"Excuse me, sir. Can I ask you a question?"

The missionary squinted at Tom like a man who needed glasses, but he smiled in an encouraging way. "Of course, young man. Ask away."

Tom cleared his throat. "My friend..." He pointed at Nathan who was avidly watching from a short distance away. "He said you told them a story last night about a healer and a baby who died."

"Ah, yes," the missionary said. A wistful look passed over his face. "Poor couple. They were very upset. But then all ended well, eh?"

Tom's heart picked up pace. "Then it's true? He really saved the baby?"

"I tend to think the couple was mistaken," the missionary said. "The baby might have been sick, but more likely unconscious than dead. But then..." The missionary lifted his thin shoulders. "The Lord does raise the dead occasionally, doesn't he? Lazarus, the centurion's servant, have you read your Bible, son?"

"Yes, sir," Tom answered, and the truth was on his side. Every Christmas Eve his mother liked him to read out loud the story of Jesus's birth.

"Then you know," the missionary said. "All believers will one day be resurrected. It's the promise of our Lord."

"But how did the healer do it?" Tom persisted. "Do you have any idea what words he said?"

The missionary gazed at Tom with a pitying kind of look. "They're heathens, you understand."

"Yes, sir," Tom said impatiently.

"That's why the Lord sent me there, to bring them into his fold."

"Yes, sir, I understand," Tom said. "But still..." He cast around for a better idea. "I'm doing a Sunday School report. I want to talk about you and the work you're doing. But I need to give them all the facts. So, if you remember what he said..."

"No, young man, I'm sorry," the missionary said. "I only know the Lord's words by heart."

4

Tom trudged along home with his parents. They lived just a few blocks from the church and when the weather was nice they always walked.

He was surprised to hear footsteps running behind him. Even more surprised to see Billy Jane.

"Hi, Mr. and Mrs. Robey," she said.

Tom's parents greeted her, then Tom saw his mother give his father a look.

"We'll see you at home," she said, smiling at Tom. She murmured something to Tom's father, then tugged on his arm to keep on walking.

As soon as they were alone, Billy Jane got right to the point. "Do you believe it?"

Tom didn't have to ask her what.

"I don't know," he said.

"I do," said Billy Jane. "I saw something like that in a book."

Billy Jane was the biggest reader Tom knew. She loved books almost as much as animals. Every Saturday she checked out the maximum number of books from the Macon library, and she read them all by the following Saturday when she checked out more.

"Let's go after school tomorrow," she said. "I'll find it again."

5

Tom felt foolish doing it, in case it was all an elaborate hoax, but he spent time looking through his mother's cookware for some kind of a pot with a hole in the lid.

There was the pressure cooker she used for canning when she made jam, but she'd skin him alive if she found out he cooked Sargent's bones in it.

If he was even going to do this. It sounded so far-fetched, he constantly talked himself out of it. Would he really dig up their old dead dog? What if it there was still flesh on his bones? He had been dead several years now, but Tom had no idea how quickly a body decomposed. He might open up the grave and find maggots and a half-eaten corpse. What if it smelled like rotting meat? His mother would be horrified at what he'd done.

By the time Tom went to bed, he wasn't sure what he would do, but he was still no closer to finding the kind of pot Nathan described.

By the next afternoon, it seemed he wouldn't need it.

Billy Jane walked through the library with the kind of ownership Tom felt toward Stilt's Pond. Complete familiarity, the confidence of knowing exactly what to do and where to go. Soon she had searched through the card catalog and remembered which book she wanted.

"It's about a Russian pilgrim," she whispered as they went to the relevant shelf.

"Why would you read that?" Tom asked.

Billy Jane gave him a look as if it was obvious. "I'm going to read every book in here."

Tom gazed at her in wonder. It was like saying she was going to fish in every body of water in the state, everything from puddles up to lakes.

The two of them sat at a table far in the back and opened the old tattered book.

Billy Jane flipped through the pages, searching for the passage. Once she found it, she pressed her finger to the paragraph as she passed the book to Tom.

He read it, then read it again.

The process was almost exactly the way Nathan described.

That alone worried him.

"What if Nathan read this book?" he asked. "And just said it was what the missionary told him?"

Billy Jane scoffed. "Mrs. Linn told me no one has checked this out in at least thirty years. Sometimes I'm the only person who has checked out a book *ever*."

Mrs. Linn was the librarian, and obviously a reliable source.

Tom read through the paragraph a third time. Billy Jane got up briefly and returned with a slip of paper and a short yellow pencil. She copied down the words from the book. Then she smiled at Tom and handed him the slip of paper and said, "I want to be there when you do it."

6

The Russian pilgrim used a different kind of pot. He described it as *earthen*, and Billy Jane pointed out that a flower pot would be perfect. "It has a hole in the bottom. And we can put foil over the top to keep it covered."

Tom always knew she was smart. But it wasn't just good grades. She had more ideas every five minutes than he could come up with in a whole day.

He found several unused flower pots out in the shed. He and Billy Jane looked them over, wondering what size they needed.

"Do you think you should use *all* of the bones?" she asked.

"Probably," Tom said. In the book the pilgrim used all

sorts of different animal bones, from bird bones to whatever other kinds he could find in the forest.

Billy Jane pointed at the largest pot. "Then we'll probably need that one."

"That's a big hole to dig," said Tom, who had recent experience to draw from.

Instead he chose one of the medium-sized pots. "Remember, we have to grind the bones anyway," Tom said. "That will take up less room."

It was going to be a long, maybe difficult process.

But the fact that Billy Jane wanted to do it with him made it a lot easier.

"Should we do it tonight?" she asked, almost in a whisper.

"Why not?" Tom said. If it worked, he wanted Rip back alive as soon as possible.

If it worked.

He still wasn't sure that this whole thing was real. Even the Russian pilgrim might have been lying. Just because something was in a book didn't make it true.

And he could just see Nathan Weaver laughing at him if he ever found out. Telling all the kids at school how gullible Tom was. *"You actually dug up your old dead dog? That's disgusting!"*

But Billy Jane believed it. And that gave Tom a certain amount of faith.

It was Monday, a school night, so Billy Jane wouldn't

be able to stay too long. She told her parents she was having dinner with the Robeys, which was true. Tom's mother was only too happy to include Billy Jane at dinner. She switched from leftovers to spaghetti and meatballs since they had a guest.

Tom's mother kept shooting his father significant looks all during dinner, but Tom forced himself to ignore them. His plans were too important to worry about his mother getting the wrong idea. He would explain to her later that Billy Jane was just a friend.

It was still light out after dinner. The sun wasn't going to set until nearly 8:30. Billy Jane's mother wanted her home before then.

"So you'll walk me home," Billy Jane told him, "and then I'll pretend to go to bed, and I'll come right back."

"I don't want you to get into trouble."

"I won't," she said. "My parents sleep like they're dead. They'll never find out."

For now, by the light of the yellow and orange sunset, they walked out to the two maple trees and surveyed where they would dig.

Billy Jane said she would use one of the shovels too. She'd helped her dad in the yard before.

"We have to do it quietly," Tom told her. "I can't let my parents hear."

"Tell them you remembered you wanted to put Rip's

favorite toy in his grave," Billy Jane said. "You have to do it tonight or you'll never sleep."

"Yeah... okay," Tom said. He was amazed at how Billy Jane's mind worked. "Then we'll both dig at the same time so they only hear the sound of one shovel."

"Good idea," Billy Jane said. Tom appreciated the praise.

They brought out the flower pot and set it in position. To grind the bones Tom had a large smooth rock that fit neatly in his hand. Billy Jane would break up the bones with the blade of a garden trowel, and Tom would do the grinding.

They carried over logs from the woodpile and gathered dry twigs and old newspapers out of the trash to act as tinder.

The two of them stood back to examine their work.

Billy Jane looked up at the darkening sky. "You should walk me home now. I'll go say goodbye to your parents."

She thanked Tom's mother for the delicious dinner. Tom could see how much his mother liked that.

As Tom left to walk Billy Jane home he could hear his parents softly laughing.

7

It was close to ten o'clock before Billy Jane came back. By then Tom had dug down to the top of Sargent's bones. He stopped digging as soon as his shovel hit something hard. He wanted to leave some of the shoveling to Billy Jane if she still wanted to.

But just to make sure, he bent down and brushed away some of the dirt in case it was something he didn't want Billy Jane to have to see. To his relief there was no rotting, decomposing meat. Just bare bones that looked yellow under the glow of the full moon.

Tom watched Billy Jane's flashlight beam grow closer.

"Hi," she whispered.

"Hi."

She was wearing jeans and sneakers and a dark cotton

blouse. Her hair was back in a headband, ready for her to work.

"Sorry I'm so late," Billy Jane whispered. "I'm glad you got started."

Tom showed her the first of the bones. He finished uncovering it and pulled it out of the dirt. It was about a foot long and might have belonged to a leg.

Billy Jane looked a little nervous as he held it in front of her. She leaned forward and sniffed it. It seemed like a good idea. Tom did the same.

It smelled a little like one of the beef bones he used to give Rip to chew, still full of marrow he'd spend hours working out with his tongue.

This bone was hard and thick like that. Not brittle and easy to break.

Not at all the way it sounded like in the Russian pilgrim's book.

Tom mentioned that to Billy Jane. She thought about it for a moment.

"The pilgrim found all those bones already on top of the ground in the forest," she said. "Maybe they were already brittle because they were exposed to the air."

Tom tried to crack the bone apart first with the garden trowel, then with his larger shovel. But it was like trying to break open a walnut with the tip of a pencil. The bone wasn't even close to fragile enough that Tom would be able to chop it up in smaller pieces and then grind it.

He sat back on his heels, discouraged.

"So we won't use all the bones," Billy Jane said. "Just a few of them. And that way we can use one of the smaller pots. Come on, we can still do this." She tugged on his sleeve and started for the shed.

Tom appreciated her optimism. He didn't want to give up, either. If there was even the slightest possibility that what the missionary and the Russian pilgrim both said was true, Tom absolutely wanted to try.

They picked out the only small pot that wasn't cracked and brought it back to the grave. Tom already had a big section of foil he'd gotten from his mother's kitchen drawer. He folded it up smaller to fit the rim of the substitute pot.

Then he and Billy Jane picked out the bones that they would burn.

"That thick one will take too long," he said. "It's like a Yule log."

In the pilgrim book, the ground-up bones burned down to an oily reddish-black tar in twenty-four hours.

Tom doubted that he had twenty-four hours. He couldn't keep the fire burning while he was at school. At most he could hope the coals would keep the flower pot hot for a few extra hours after he stopped adding wood.

At last everything was in place: one of his mother's canning jars down at the bottom of the hole, the flower pot sitting on top of it, a collection of small bones inside it, and the foil tightly covering the top.

He balled up the newspapers and set twigs all around and lit a match.

He and Billy Jane squatted near the little fire and took turns adding more tinder. Before long the flames were circled all around the pot.

"Tom?" his mother's voice called from the back of the house.

"Hide!" Tom whispered.

Billy Jane was already ducking behind one of the maples when Tom's mother started across the yard.

"What ever are you doing?" she asked.

He jumped to his feet and hurried forward to meet her.

The words leapt to his tongue. "I decided I'd like to sleep out here tonight," he said. "Please, Mom. Just this once. I just want to say goodbye to Rip."

"Oh, honey." She reached out and ran her fingers through the top of his hair. Tom cringed at the gesture. It was something she used to do when he was a little kid.

Not something he wanted Billy Jane to see. Like his mother still treated him like a baby.

"Please, Mom," he said again.

"It's a school night," she said.

"I know, but I can't sleep without him yet. I know I'll be able to sleep if I stay out here."

He could see her hesitating. His mother had a soft heart, especially where animals were concerned.

"You promise you won't stay up all night?" she asked.

"Promise."

She set one hand on her hip. "All right, but just tonight. You run in and get your sleeping bag and a pillow. You can't sleep on the bare ground."

Tom didn't wait for more discussion. He ran into the house, knowing Billy Jane would stay hidden behind the tree.

He pulled his rolled-up sleeping bag off the upper shelf in his closet and took his pillow off the bed. His mother was waiting for him when he got back to the kitchen. She held out a flashlight, which he was glad to take. He didn't realize he'd want one until Billy Jane showed up with hers.

"Thanks, Mom."

She patted his shoulder and he ran back outside to the fire. It was time to feed it more wood.

8

____

Around eleven, Billy Jane was having a hard time staying awake.

She lay down on the dirt with her hands folded underneath her cheek. Tom debated whether to offer her his pillow. It might not smell very good, since he sometimes drooled on it during the night. He'd hate for her to smell it and think he was disgusting.

What he really needed to do was walk her home. Even though he wanted her company. But he couldn't have her staying out until midnight. What if her parents woke up after all and found that she was gone?

He gently rocked her shoulder.

She sat up and brushed the dirt from her hair.

"I should walk you home now," Tom said.

Billy Jane didn't argue.

She opened the corner of the foil to take a peek inside. Tom looked, too.

A meaty-smelling smoke escaped from the top. The bones looked like they might be softening.

It was interesting, in a way, but then he remembered these weren't just any bones, they once belonged to Sargent. And that made him think of Rip, lying dead in the nearby grave.

He smoothed the foil back over the top.

They added a few more pieces of wood to burn while Tom was away. Then they set out by moonlight and flashlight to walk the block and a half to Billy Jane's house.

She led him around to the side where three steps climbed up to the door.

"Good luck," she whispered. "I'll come over before school tomorrow. Wait for me."

She gave his hand a squeeze and ran up the steps.

All the way home Tom thought about that squeeze. What it meant. If anything.

Was it just a friendly gesture? Or was it her way of saying she liked him?

Or was it just that she was enthusiastic about their project? She would have squeezed even Nathan Weaver's hand out of excitement.

Tom returned to tending his fire. He stirred the orange coals with a stick, then added a few thin logs.

Then he unrolled his sleeping bag and set his pillow

on top and crawled inside. He might take a little nap for a while and get up in an hour or so to add more wood.

Birdsong woke him.

The fire had burned out, but the ashes were still warm. The flower pot was cool enough to touch.

He tilted it to the side to check the canning jar below.

A thin smear of dark liquid covered the glass bottom.

Tom grinned.

He checked the bones in the pot. There were still solid-looking, but much whiter than they seemed by moonlight last night.

Billy Jane arrived while he was examining them.

She looked fresh and clean in her plaid skirt, white blouse, rolled-down white bobby socks, and penny loafers. She wore her shoulder-length brown hair pulled back in a headband. He bet her breath smelled like toothpaste.

Tom hadn't even been inside his house yet to wash up. He probably smelled like smoke and bad breath. So he kept a certain distance, but he was still anxious to show Billy Jane what was in the jar.

She laughed and looked at him bright-eyed. "It worked!"

He put the jar back under the pot and added small pieces of wood around it to stoke up the fire again. "I'm going to let it burn the whole twenty-four hours and get as much liquid as we can."

"Good," said Billy Jane. "Then we can do the rest of it tonight."

The rest of it.

Pouring it over Rip's grave and bringing that good dog back to life.

9

Tom's mother wouldn't let him sleep outside again. He had to sneak out after his parents went to bed.

He realized it wasn't right for Billy Jane to walk to his house alone, so he told her after school to wait for him this time.

She told him which window was her bedroom. It was after eleven when he tapped on it.

She came bounding down the steps just a few minutes later. They set off quickly for Tom's house.

"Did you check it?" she asked.

"Not yet," he said. "I thought we could look together."

He'd added more wood all afternoon once he got home from school.

"What are you burning out there?" his mother asked.

"Rip's toys," he lied.

His mother looked at him strangely.

"Billy Jane said the vet told her about it. He said it helps get over the loss of a pet."

Tom's mother got a sad look in her eyes. He hated to lie to her, but he had to do it.

"I miss him, too," she said. Her eyes were misting up. She reached over to run her fingers through Tom's hair, but he dodged her in time.

"I'll be done tonight," Tom said. "Then I can really say goodbye."

What was he going to tell her if Rip suddenly sprang back to life? How was he going to explain?

He would worry about that later.

Right now he just hoped with all his heart that it worked.

When they checked the jar, there was about half an inch of a foul-smelling liquid. It looked thick enough to qualify as tar.

"Okay," Tom said, his voice breathier than normal. He could feel his heartbeat starting to race.

Billy Jane reached over and squeezed his hand again. He smiled at her and she nervously smiled back.

Tom wasn't nervous. He felt brave. Brave and ready to do what came next.

He pulled out of his pocket the slip of paper Billy Jane

had written on in the library. He had read it so many times since then, he could probably say the words from memory, but this was too important to leave to chance.

They moved over to Rip's grave. The dirt on top looked darker and looser than Sargent's older grave.

Tom scooped down through the top of the soil and made a little well.

Billy Jane held the jar poised over the grave, ready for Tom to say the words.

He cleared his throat.

"Love of creation," he began. "O create. Love of living. O give life."

The words were strange, but the Russian pilgrim lived a long time ago, and maybe they talked that way.

"Life shall ever have dominion over death," he went on, "and the pure in heart shall know Thee by your hand."

Billy Jane waited, wide-eyed. Her hand looked frozen where it held the jar.

Tom nodded to her solemnly.

Billy Jane gently tipped out the liquid.

It flowed thick like fudge over a sundae. Billy Jane shook out the last few drops.

Then Tom folded the loose dirt over the top of it, filling in the well.

The two of them knelt beside the grave and waited.

Tom was afraid to breathe.

The light from the full moon had been shining down on their ceremony up to now, but an instant later a cloud moved across it and shrouded them in darkness.

"Tom?" Billy Jane whispered.

He continued holding his breath and couldn't answer.

He felt her hand clasping his. That was fine. He held on and waited for what would happen.

A strong wind blew toward them from his house with enough power to ruffle Tom's hair. Loose dirt from the top of Rip's grave gusted into the air.

Billy Jane gave a little yelp and held on tighter.

The wind gathered around Tom and Billy Jane and the graves like they were at the center of a spinning carnival ride.

Tom closed his eyes.

He thought he could feel something brushing lightly against his arms.

A slight weight on top of his thighs.

The soft squirming of a small furry body.

The milk-sour smell of a puppy's breath.

Tom gasped and opened his eyes.

He could have sworn he saw a shape made of smoke.

He turned to Billy Jane, but she was staring straight ahead to exactly where Tom had been looking a moment before.

"Did you see it?" she whispered.

Tom's heart pounded.

"See what?" He needed to make sure.

Billy Jane released Tom's hand and pantomimed the size and shape.

"A puppy," she whispered in awe.

Tom swallowed hard. "Yeah. I think I saw it."

The wind curdled around them one last time, and then it died as quickly as it rose.

The cloud moved aside, and the moon shone brightly once more.

Tom and Billy Jane looked at each other.

Then they both looked at Rip's grave.

Tom expected to see the dirt bursting up as Rip dug himself to the surface.

But they waited. And waited.

At last Tom couldn't stand it. He got the shovel and dug down himself.

If Rip was alive but too buried in dirt, maybe it was up to Tom to free him.

But once he dug deep enough, he knew he was close to Rip's body.

He couldn't stand hitting him with the blade of the shovel. Instead he knelt beside the hole and called.

"Rip? Rip boy?"

"Rip," Billy Jane joined in.

There was a break in her voice. In another moment, she was crying.

"I thought it worked," she said.

"So did I," Tom answered. He felt a horrible pain in his chest.

They waited a little while longer. Billy Jane cried until it was time to walk her home.

10

Tom moved through the day in a sort of daze, unsure if what he thought happened last night really did.

The shape made out of smoke. The feeling of soft fur and the warm weight of a small living body.

The irresistible smell of a puppy's breath.

Had it all been in his head?

But it was in Billy Jane's head, too, or else it really did happen the way they both saw it. They ate their sandwiches outside together at lunch so they could go over it several more times.

They each took turns describing exactly what they remembered.

When Tom described holding the puppy, Billy Jane's eyes teared up again.

"I wish I could have felt that," she said. "But I saw it, and I swear I could hear it panting."

"Do you think we scared it away?" Tom said. He couldn't remember making any fast motions, but he might have forgotten.

Billy Jane shook her head. "We were both as still as statues. Once the wind started, I don't think either of us ever moved."

"Then what do you think it all was?" Tom asked. "Why didn't Rip come back?"

Billy Jane sighed. "We must have gotten it only half right. We're such amateurs. I bet a real Congo healer could have done it."

It wasn't the answer Tom wanted. He needed to fix this now.

"I think we should try again," he said. "Start over and do it again."

Billy Jane crumpled her sandwich paper and got up from the low seat wall in the back of the school.

"I agree," she said. "We got so close. I know we can do it next time."

"But what *was* it?" Tom asked again as they walked together back inside.

She suddenly stopped and clutched his arm. "Oh my gosh, that's it."

She softly repeated the familiar sound they'd both heard Nathan Weaver make a few days before.

The crying sound of a baby.

"Maybe they all start over," she said. "Whether they're a baby or an adult." She smiled, sure she had the answer. "Rip isn't coming back like he was, he's coming back as a *puppy*."

11

As they walked down Vine Street after school, making plans for how to do it right this time, Billy Jane suddenly drew in a sharp breath.

She pointed to the street.

"Tom, that's him."

A rusted red truck with a busted left tail light was turning right into the parking lot of the Bungalow Café.

A red mist seemed to cloud Tom's eyes.

A flash of hatred overtook his mind.

He took off at a run. Billy Jane called to him, then started running too.

He was down the block and across the street so fast it was like some sprinter had possessed his body.

"Tom! Tom!" Billy Jane cried. "What are you going to do?"

He didn't answer because he didn't know. He stood in the parking lot for a moment to catch his breath, then opened the door to the Bungalow Café and went inside.

He didn't get a good look at the man when he left his truck, other than to notice he wore a dark shirt.

Tom scanned the people on the stools at the counter, then looked to his left at the row of booths.

A loud laugh reached his ears. Something about the sound of that voice made him hurt. He found the dark-shirted man sitting with two friends in the second-to-last booth.

Billy Jane caught Tom's arm. "Those men are big," she warned him.

Tom didn't care. Right was right. He strode fearlessly to the booth.

"Is that your red truck?" he asked the laughing man.

The man wasn't laughing now.

"What if it is?" he said.

"Then mister, you killed my dog."

Conversations stopped. Tom's voice had come out louder than he expected. But he didn't care, he stood his ground. Hatred steeled his spine.

The man looked about Tom's parents' age. He had black hair slicked back from his forehead. He wore tan workpants and a plaid short-sleeved, button-down shirt. His arms looked tan and muscular like maybe he worked on machinery or did some other kind of physical labor.

He sat alone on his side of the booth. Now he scooted to the end and stood up.

He was at least a foot taller than Tom. But Tom stared him down like they were the same size.

People in the café were watching.

The man seemed to notice that too.

"Come talk to me outside," he said to Tom.

Without waiting for agreement, the man headed for the door.

"No, Tom," Billy Jane pleaded as he passed her. "Please don't get in a fight."

Tom had only been in one fight ever before, and that was when he was eight.

It was a lot of pushing and rolling around. Neither of them threw a punch.

He didn't know what the red truck man would do. If it was a real fight, Tom knew he would lose.

But to just drive over someone's dog and not even stop.

To kill Rip and not even care.

If Tom didn't stand up for something like that, he'd feel like a coward the rest of his life.

He only hoped the man wouldn't hit him too hard.

And that he could hit the man hard enough himself.

The man stood waiting at the side of the red truck.

"What's your name, boy?"

Tom glared at him. He didn't have to answer.

"I'm Ray Swadley," the man said, sticking out his hand.

People were coming out of the café to watch. Including Ray Swadley's two mean-looking friends.

Billy Jane was watching too. She stood with her hands clasped together in front of her mouth. Her eyes were wide with fright.

Ray lowered his outstretched hand. He glanced over at the crowd and then turned his back to them.

"When was this?" he said.

For a moment Tom didn't understand what he was asking.

"Friday," Tom said.

Ray Swadley gave a heavy sigh.

He looked back toward his two friends, then faced Tom again and reached into his back pocket. He pulled out his wallet.

"Look, I'm real sorry," he said. "But it wasn't me. Someone borrowed my truck."

He pulled out a ten-dollar bill and handed it to Tom.

Tom had no desire to take it.

Ray Swadley sighed again. He added another ten.

When Tom made no move to take them, Ray pushed them into his palm.

"I've got a dog," Ray said. "So I know. I'm real sorry. Nothing else I can do."

He went to pat Tom's shoulder, but Tom flinched away.

The anger had no place to go. It was still a hurricane inside his head.

Money was no substitute for a dog. Money was no apology for death.

That was what he wanted, Tom realized. Something more than just *I'm real sorry.*

"Do you even care?" he asked Ray Swadley as the man headed back to eat with his friends.

"I got my own problems," Ray said. "They're a lot bigger than yours."

The crowd wandered back inside, clearly disappointed there wasn't a fight.

Billy Jane looked wilted and tired. She came over as soon as Ray left.

Tears shone in her eyes. "I'm proud of you."

The tension started to make itself known in Tom's body. He could feel his hands and legs shake.

He nodded, not trusting his voice not to shake too.

He turned back toward Vine and walked hard.

"How much did he give you?" Billy Jane asked in a while.

Tom showed her the two ten-dollar bills still stuffed in his hand.

Billy Jane made a *pfff* of disapproval. He glanced at her. She was all right.

By the time they got back to Tom's house, he felt as dry and depleted as a husk. He greeted his mother and invited Billy Jane to take a seat while he got out two glasses and the pitcher of lemonade.

"How was school today?" his mother asked.

Tom and Billy Jane exchanged a look.

"Fine," Tom said.

"Good," Billy Jane answered.

The two of them sat at the kitchen table and drained their glasses.

"Oh, Tom," his mother said, "I wanted to tell you. I was talking to Mrs. Doughty today. You'll never guess."

The Doughtys lived out on five acres at the west end of town. Their daughter Beth was a year younger than Tom.

"Their dog Sadie just had a litter."

Tom jerked his head up, alert.

Billy Jane sat up straight. "What kind?"

"Labrador Retriever, same as Rip."

Tom was out of his chair in a flash.

"If you wait till your dad gets home, he can drive you," his mother said.

"That's all right," Tom said. Billy Jane was close at his heels.

"Be home for supper," his mother called, but Tom and Billy Jane were already running.

Mrs. Doughty was a stout, friendly woman with thick rough hands. Her daughter Beth looked like she'd grow up to be just the same.

"Eight of 'em are already spoken for," Mrs. Doughty said. "But there's still that little girl over there and one of those boys rolling in the grass."

All of the puppies were black. Some explored the vast backyard on their own, while two of them tumbled and played with each other near a rose bush close to the house. Their bright white teeth flashed as they growled in mock fight.

Billy Jane was already sitting cross-legged on the lawn, holding the girl puppy Mrs. Doughty pointed out. Soon Beth Doughty came out to join her.

Billy Jane lifted the puppy to her face and rubbed her

cheek against the soft fur. The girl dog bit the tip of her nose. Billy Jane laughed.

"Aww, I wish I could have one!" she said.

"Your daddy lets you keep dogs," Beth said.

"I know, but he says we already have too many animals," Billy Jane said with a sigh. "But just one more! She's so sweet."

"It's the smaller one," Mrs. Doughty said to Tom as he headed over to the wrestling puppies. "The bigger one's going to Jed Jepson."

Tom extracted the smaller of the two boys and turned him around to look at his face.

The dog looked directly into his eyes.

A lump sprang into Tom's throat.

He sat on the grass and held the puppy on his lap. And knew in the instant that he had done this before.

Not just with Rip seven years ago, but with a puppy made of smoke last night.

Tom closed his eyes. He could smell the puppy's milk-sour breath. Feel the warmth and weight of his squirming body. Feel the love he still felt for Rip.

Was this Rip, come back to him? But it wasn't possible, Rip was still alive when these puppies were born.

How did any of this work? Was it magic, was it a miracle, or was it just a coincidence that he wanted to turn into something more?

He looked across the lawn to where Billy Jane held

her puppy across one shoulder like a mother with her baby. She stroked the puppy's back. It looked like the dog was fast asleep.

Tom got up and carried his puppy over to Mrs. Doughty. He kept his voice quiet as he asked her the price.

"Ten dollar each," Mrs. Doughty said.

Tom handed her Ray Swadley's bills.

He carried his puppy over to the girls and asked Billy Jane if she was ready to go back home.

She got a sad look on her face. She started to hand her sleeping puppy to Beth.

"No, her too," Tom said. "I bought them both."

Beth yelped with delight. Billy Jane looked at him in amazement. A smile broke across her pretty face. "Oh, Tom." There were tears shining in her eyes again, but this time they went with the smile.

They both thanked Mrs. Doughty and carried their puppies off toward the road.

Neither of them spoke for what felt like a long time.

"Tom, thank you," Billy Jane said at last. "I'll love her so much."

She hugged the little black body to her chest.

Tom carried his dog more like a sack of potatoes, cradled in both arms and resting against his stomach.

"What should we call them?" Billy Jane asked.

Tom already knew. He knew back when he first picked up the pup.

"Mine's Smoky," he said. It felt right. He couldn't imagine what else he could possibly call him.

"Mine's Stella," Billy Jane said. She bumped her arm against Tom's. He didn't move away, he moved closer to her.

That felt right too.

Back at his house they set the two puppies to play in the grass. Billy Jane and Tom's mother supervised them for a while so Tom could go take care of the rest.

He dismantled his earthen oven. Put the cooked bones back in Sargent's grave and smoothed dirt back on top. He stirred the ashes left over from the fire and buried them with more dirt back into the hole.

He paused for a minute near Rip's grave.

Then he sat down for a quiet chat.

He went through all the memories he wanted to hold, from the time Rip the puppy first looked him in the eye.

All the adventures the two of them had. The good fishing. The many hunts with Tom and his dad.

The way Rip stuck near Tom any time they were out together. How he could have chosen Tom's dad instead, but he picked Tom to be his true master.

His true friend.

Tom felt the same way about Rip.

"Thank you," he whispered to his dog. "You were the best, Rip. I mean it."

He patted the top of Rip's grave and imagined he might be patting the top of Rip's head.

Laughter reached his ears. Billy Jane was lying on the grass while the two puppies crawled all over her.

If Smoky could be even half the dog that Rip was.

Or maybe like Rip, and even better.

No dog was a substitute for another. They were all exactly the dogs they were.

Tom gave Rip's head one final pat, then went off to be with the next one.

the Slip of a Rib

1

Winnie Parsons stood at the granite-topped island in her kitchen and pressed her palms into a soft round lump of dough. She had awakened in the mood for bread. Not just for the taste of it, but mostly for the smell of a yeasty loaf baking in the oven, warming the whole house.

A cold February morning like today made her want to stay inside, bake, eat, sit by the fire with a mug of coffee or hot chocolate, and read. Her yellow Labrador, Clover, had different ideas of what was fun, and so Winnie had walked her on the nearby University of Arizona campus first to let the dog frolic on the frost-covered grass.

But now Clover was curled up on her dog bed beside the crackling fire, and Winnie could fulfill her urge to bake. There were a few steps between here and a hot, finished loaf, but Winnie's part in it was short. Just mix a few ingredients, knead, then let the dough sit covered by a dishtowel all day in the warmth of the kitchen window. Even in winter, the sun shone through golden onto one particular spot on the counter. The dough would be ready to bake by midafternoon.

Winnie's cell phone rang. Her hands were still deep in dough. She might have let the call go to voicemail, if not for the name she saw on her screen.

She used her relatively clean pinky finger to press the button to put the call on her phone's speaker.

Dr. Amanda Birkauer was usually in a hurry, and this morning was no exception.

"Got an interesting call just now," said Amanda without any greeting or other preamble. Winnie didn't mind. She liked her friend's ability to cut right to it, leave out the fluff, get to the interesting parts sooner.

Amanda had been Winnie's colleague in the University of Arizona Psychology department when Winnie was a professor there. Winnie—Dr. Winifred Parsons—had retired four years ago, but her decades-long friendship with Amanda endured.

They had another connection as well. Amanda Birkauer was the Assistant Director of the university's mind lab, better known as the parapsychology lab.

Winnie was a frequent test subject there. As a clairvoyant and occasional medical intuitive, Winnie wanted both to share her knowledge and to learn more about her gifts herself. She thought of them as any talent, like the ability to play chess or to do the high jump. She had been born clairvoyant, but she could still grow and improve the more she practiced.

And the more she learned from Amanda's scientists and from other psychics who visited the lab, the more Winnie understood what she might be capable of if she expanded what she thought of as even possible.

"Remember Penny Bristol?" Amanda asked.

Winnie smoothed her dough into a ball and thought for a moment. "No." But as soon as she said it, an image flashed in her mind: of an elderly woman, well-dressed and obviously wealthy, pushing a rolling walker that had a cargo basket on top. A soft blue blanket lined the basket, and a small brown and white dog rode nestled inside.

"King Arthur!" Winnie said, smiling.

"The one," Amanda confirmed over the speaker.

It must have been five or six years ago. Mrs. Penny Bristol had brought her Cavalier King Charles Spaniel, named King Arthur, to the parapsychology lab to see if anyone could read the little dog's mind.

Winnie had been on her way out of one of the rooms where she'd participated in whatever new test Amanda and her lab assistants had cooked up for her that day.

Winnie came to a sudden halt in front of the woman

and her dog. She hadn't planned on stopping—she had her own work to do, and needed to get back to her office —but something about the dog tugged at her and made her want to stay.

"Well, hello there." Winnie smiled at the spaniel and reached out to pet its soft head between the two long ears that hung over the lip of the basket.

The dog growled at Winnie and bared his small teeth.

"Arthur! Stop that!" Mrs. Bristol seemed embarrassed. "He's normally never like this," she said by way of apology. And then tears misted her eyes. "I ... I don't know what to do with him. Something has happened. He's not himself anymore."

A phrase had come to Winnie's mind. A phrase and an image.

"He has a rib out," Winnie told Mrs. Bristol. "On his left side. He's been in terrible pain for over a week. He's sorry, but he hasn't known how else to tell you."

Mrs. Bristol gaped at Winnie. "How ... how..."

Winnie waved the question away. "If you take him to your vet this morning, I'm sure they can fix it right away."

Mrs. Bristol had gripped Winnie's hand. "Thank you, oh thank you!"

Amanda came out of the lab then just in time to see the end of their conversation. Winnie gave her a nod, then hurried off toward the stairs leading up to her floor.

"Who was that?" Mrs. Bristol asked.

"I'm sorry," Winnie could hear Amanda tell the woman, "but we keep our test subjects' identities confidential."

Winnie was there that morning in her capacity as Test Subject number 2134, not as Professor Winifred Parsons.

She appreciated Amanda's discretion. Most of Winnie's colleagues had no idea she was clairvoyant. Winnie suspected that many of them would not handle it well. Although the university's mind lab was well-respected among others pursuing that same research, some scientists still viewed parapsychology as a fringe subject, not worthy of serious study—and even less worthy of funding.

Winnie had already risen high through the ranks of the Psychology department by then, even acting as Chair of the department for a while. She wrote many well-respected articles and textbooks in her field of Consumer Psychology. Her students and colleagues thought of her as a typical academic.

So although Winnie was happy to help Mrs. Bristol and King Arthur solve their problem in the moment, she did not want to see them up on her own floor, Mrs. Bristol smiling in her office doorway, loudly thanking her for reading the little dog's mind.

And besides, Winnie hadn't read the dog's mind. That

wasn't how she received the information. Instead she saw a flashed image of the misplaced rib, and heard a phrase in her own voice telling her everything else she conveyed to Mrs. Bristol.

"So what do the two of them need now?" Winnie asked Amanda.

"Nothing," Amanda said. "Penny Bristol died about three months ago—"

"Oh, I'm sorry to hear that."

"—and believe it or not, she left you some money."

"She *what*?"

Amanda chuckled. "Not by name. That's why I got the call this morning. Someone at the Animal Adoption Center wanted to know who that nice white-haired lady was who told Mrs. Bristol that King Arthur had slipped a rib."

Winnie's hair was more of a natural blondish-white, but she didn't mind the description. The hair had made her look older than her years for at least a decade. Now at sixty-eight, Winnie knew that when strangers looked at her they saw an old lady. She sometimes used that to her advantage to fade unnoticed into a crowd.

"Apparently Penny left most of her money to the Animal Adoption Center. Isn't that nice?"

"It is," Winnie agreed. She thought well of anyone who used their wealth to take care of children and animals in particular.

"She also gave them a separate twenty thousand dollars specifically to spend on *you*."

"On me? Why?"

Winnie set her dough in a bowl, covered it with a clean dish towel, and positioned the bowl on the counter beneath the sunny kitchen window.

She quickly washed the flour from her hands, then took Amanda off speaker. Winnie was tired of shouting.

She took the phone to the bedroom to retrieve her headset for a more comfortable call. Then she returned to the living room and sat on the thick Asian rug next to Clover, leaning against the warm fireplace hearth.

"Don't make me drag it out of you," Winnie said. "Just start at the beginning."

"Hold on."

Winnie could hear Amanda cover the phone with her hand and speak to someone who had come into her office. Winnie was always amazed at Amanda's ability to juggle so many demands at once: teaching, running the lab, and writing new academic articles every few months to share her lab's findings with the international scientific community.

Amanda was fifty-three, a full fifteen years younger than Winnie, but even in her twenties and thirties, Winnie never had Amanda's kind of energy or her ability to multitask.

And in Amanda's spare time, what there was of it, she

trained as a tri-athlete. Winnie certainly never had that much extra energy to burn.

Some people were just made differently. Winnie enjoyed watching her friend manage her busy life and career, but she preferred watching it from the quiet and calm of her own slower life.

Like right now. Winnie added another log to the fire, then settled back next to Clover. She petted the dog and patiently waited for Amanda to return to the call. The dog groaned as Winnie scratched behind her ears, then Clover sank even more deeply into her plush green bed.

"Sorry," Amanda said. "I have to go in a sec. Here's the short version. Penny gave them twenty thousand to spend on that nice white-haired psychic lady from the U of A if they ever need to solve any behavioral issues. You're supposed to be the pet guru now, I guess."

"I don't mean to sound ungrateful," Winnie said, "but don't you think they should call Chandra instead?" Winnie had met the woman several years before at Amanda's lab. Chandra actually was an intuitive pet communicator.

"She specifically left the money for you," Amanda said. "It's in her will. The Animal Adoption Center is emailing me a copy any minute."

Winnie sighed. "Okay, so what do I do?"

"They need you. They're doing a Valentine's Weekend

Adopt-a-thon, and they want to place as many animals as they can."

"But that's this weekend," Winnie said. "Awfully short notice."

"I think it took them a while to figure out how to find you. But it sounds like now they're desperate. Some of their animals are pretty shut down. They're hoping you can come out there and find out what all of them need so the Center can get them to their forever homes. Sounds pretty sweet, actually."

"It does," Winnie agreed. Although the responsibility of the task seemed daunting. How many animals needed her help? What if she couldn't hear them? And how was she supposed to get this done by the weekend?

Amanda told someone on her end, "Okay, I'm coming. Listen," she said to Winnie, "gotta go. I'll send you over the will later if you want it. But the person who wants you is a woman named Irma Makelski. I'll send you her info. Good luck. See you."

"See you—"

The call ended as abruptly as it started.

Winnie removed her headset and continued to sit on the floor beside Clover, running her fingers through the dog's thick winter coat.

She didn't know what to think.

On the one hand, she was touched that that short

interaction so many years ago had made Mrs. Bristol remember Winnie in her will.

On the other hand, Winnie couldn't be certain that she would be able to communicate with any of the other animals at the shelter. It was not a skill she practiced. She didn't even speak with Clover that way. The two of them had a close relationship, but Clover spoke with her eyes and her wagging tail, not by sending Winnie images and messages.

Although maybe it was only because Winnie never tried to reach out to her that way.

She closed her eyes. Took a deep and clearing breath. Then she opened her eyes and watched for Clover's reaction as Winnie spoke in her mind to the dog.

Clover. Are you a pretty girl?

The dog continued to sleep.

Clover, do you want a carrot?

That got the Lab to open one eye.

Clover, do you want to—

Winnie had been about to ask her if she wanted to go for a walk.

But the wind was howling and the thermometer showed it was in the forties outside, and Winnie didn't want to lie to the dog. She would not be taking Clover for a walk again today, even if it promising that might prove she could talk to the dog in her mind.

Winnie let the sleeping dog sleep. She heard her email ding.

Before running out the door to whatever demand was pulling on her next, Amanda had taken a moment to forward Winnie the will.

Winnie skipped through the formal language at the beginning, and scanned through the pages looking for the part that mentioned her.

But her eyes settled on Section 6, first. It bore the title PROVISIONS FOR THE HEALTH AND HAPPINESS OF KING ARTHUR.

So the little dog had outlived his mistress. Winnie knew that could be a tricky situation. She had already made her niece Rose swear that she and her family would adopt Clover if Winnie should exit before the dog. It gave her great peace of mind.

Mrs. Bristol had obviously sought that peace of mind as well.

Her will appointed a woman named Charlotte Amper to be King Arthur's caretaker. And Mrs. Bristol left the Amper woman a generous salary and expense allowance to see that it was properly done.

Section 6 of the will listed all the various services that should be paid for out of the estate. The list was long, but a few of them caught Winnie's eye.

Weekly grooming by someone named Pierre LeFranc, at a rate easily three times as much as Winnie spent on her own haircuts. Continued employment of the cook, Margery, who knew how to make all of the spaniel's favorite foods. Gas and upkeep for Mrs. Bristol's Cadillac so that Charlotte Amper could drive King Arthur through the foothills above Tucson and let him enjoy looking at the scenery out the window.

Winnie scrolled down to the next page where Section 6 of the will continued. When it came to her beloved dog's comfort, Mrs. Bristol had obviously tried to think of everything.

In a paragraph titled *House,* her lawyer had written a brief explanation of what his client intended. Mrs. Bristol did not want King Arthur's life to be any more upended than it would already be after his owner's death.

Therefore the executor of the estate should delay selling the house and distributing the proceeds to the designated charity. Instead, Mrs. Bristol wanted Charlotte Amper and the dog to stay in the house with all expenses paid for as long as King Arthur lived.

Suddenly Winnie didn't feel so strange about the twenty thousand dollars Mrs. Bristol had allocated to her. Instead she took it in stride.

Mrs. Bristol saw her as part of the team, along with Pierre the groomer and Margery the cook and Charlotte Amper the dog caretaker. That white-haired psychic lady had a role to play, too.

If Mrs. Bristol wanted the Animal Adoption Center to

have the resources it needed to help place more of their animals in loving homes, then Winnie was happy to help the cause.

A Valentine's Weekend Adopt-a-thon was exactly the kind of charitable event Winnie could feel good about supporting.

Now she only hoped she could justify Mrs. Bristol's faith in what Winnie could do.

2

Winnie had never visited the Animal Adoption Center. She often told herself that when the time came to get a dog or cat, she would go to the shelter and rescue the one that felt like the right match.

But the years went by, and Winnie was always too busy at work to think about bringing home a pet. She kept pushing the matter to some vague time in the future.

Her husband, Joe, had solved that by bringing home a puppy for Winnie for her sixty-first birthday. It was love at first sight. How Joe knew which puppy to choose was as much a mystery to him as it was to Winnie. Clover slipped so perfectly into their family life, it was as though she were a puzzle piece that had been missing.

Joe died just four years later. Although Winnie still missed him every day, she could only imagine how bottomlessly lonely she might have felt if she didn't still have Clover to share her life.

So although she had never followed through on her plan to visit the Animal Adoption Center, she was glad to pull up to the building now and be able to help the animals inside find homes with people who would love them the rest of their lives.

The Center was set far back from the road, so Winnie couldn't see its bright orange exterior until she drove further up the gravel driveway.

The building looked freshly painted. Maybe some of Penny Bristol's money had been spent that way. The Center must have hired an artist, too, because painted on top of the orange backdrop was a cheerful mural of dogs and cats and birds all playing together.

This was not the solemn, prison-like facility Winnie dreaded seeing. Her heart immediately lightened.

From where she parked, Winnie could see a large chain link enclosure at the back of the property. It might be as big as the building complex itself. Groups of dogs ran and played on an imitation grass surface out there, supervised by several people who must be on the staff.

Winnie entered the building, where the brightly painted colors continued inside the lobby. Each brick wall bore a different cheerful color: yellow, turquoise, sky blue, pink.

There were framed photographs covering most of the

turquoise wall. Winnie could see happy individuals and happy families hugging the pets they had adopted from the Center.

Whoever designed the look of the place knew how to make it welcoming for the visitors. From what Winnie saw so far, this did not feel like a shelter where people dumped their unwanted animals. It felt more like a boarding facility where pets waited for the right people to come along who would then whisk them off to their proper and loving homes.

A young woman in her early twenties, with shoulder-length purple hair, sat behind a front reception counter talking into a telephone headset. Winnie wondered if she colored her hair specifically to add to the cheerful ambience of the lobby. The young woman smiled at Winnie and held up a finger for her to wait while she answered a few more of the caller's questions.

As soon as the call ended, the young woman said, "Welcome! Are you here to find a pet?"

"No, actually, I'm here for an appointment with Irma."

The girl's eyes lit with excitement. "Are you that psychic?"

Winnie preferred less flashy terms—clairvoyant, gifted, intuitive—but she understood that people grouped all psi abilities into the same broad category. The word *psychic* had taken its hits over the years, especially when dial-a-psychic ads started appearing on late-night TV.

Unfortunately, there were many frauds out there who were happy to take people's money in exchange for vague pronouncements.

Someone close to you will be sick. A good guess. Everyone knew someone who succumbed to at least the common cold.

You will face unexpected difficulties in the new year, but by summer, they should all work out.

I see more, but I'm afraid our time is up. Input your credit card for another five minutes.

Winnie used to wonder how the fake psychics could live with themselves. How they could prey on other people's hopes and fears.

But her years studying psychology had put that mystery to rest. Some people were simply greedy. Some people thought if they could trick other people, it meant they were smarter than everyone else.

They didn't care who they hurt in the process. Feeling guilty never even crossed their minds.

Winnie confirmed to the purple-haired receptionist who she was. The young woman jumped up from her chair and went off through a door to her right to find Irma Makelski somewhere in back.

In that brief moment while the door was open, Winnie could hear the noise that the thick brick walls so effectively screened.

Dogs barking. And barking. Some howling. Human voices shouting over the din.

The door closed again and Winnie shivered. She could hear pain in that barking and howling.

Despite the carefully managed exterior, this place was a shelter after all. Animals had been dumped here by their thoughtless owners. Animals had been captured and brought in from the streets.

So far, the animals here had missed out on a pampered life like King Arthur's. But maybe Winnie could help them find new owners who would shower them with that kind of love.

The door behind the reception desk opened again, and a tall, thin woman with short gray hair came striding into the lobby with her hand outstretched and a smile on her weathered face.

"Mrs. Parsons."

It was Doctor Parsons, but Winnie rarely corrected people about that, either. She smiled and shook the woman's hand. "Winnie, please."

"Irma. I'm so glad you're here. Thank you for coming."

The director of the Animal Adoption Center might be Winnie's age or older. It was difficult for Winnie to tell. She had the leathery skin of someone who spent a lifetime outdoors. Winnie liked her plain and unfussy look.

The short gray hair, no makeup, no jewelry. This woman was practical and was here to work. Irma wore jeans that might have been clean at some point, but that were currently covered in dust and crusted food and what looked like a few spots of dried blood.

She wore an oversized light blue sweatshirt that bore the Animal Adoption Center logo, a circle with a floppy-eared, grinning dog in the center. It was one of the faces from the mural on the front of the building.

Despite the dirt and stains on it, the sweatshirt looked fairly new. Maybe staff clothing was another benefit of Penny Bristol's bequest. Remembering how elegantly Mrs. Bristol was dressed the day Winnie met her, Winnie had the feeling that Mrs. Bristol would approve.

Winnie was dressed just as casually as Irma. She wore long john bottoms underneath her charcoal gray hiking pants, one of Joe's old T-shirts beneath a coral-colored fleece sweater, and her navy blue fleece vest over that in case they would spend time outdoors and she needed to keep warm. On her feet she wore what she usually wore outside the house, a pair of comfortable and sturdy sneakers.

"Dog?" Irma asked, picking a few of Clover's yellow hairs off the shoulder of Winnie's dark blue vest. She studied the sample. "Labrador?"

Winnie laughed. "Oh, you're good."

"Since you're already a dog owner," Irma said, "you probably understand what you're in for here." She pointed to the various stains on her jeans and sweatshirt.

"Fancy Feast, slobber, dog vomit, blood from a broken toenail." She brushed off the back of her jeans. "Who knows what else. Can't be too fussy."

Irma smiled with radiant warmth. Winnie liked her immediately.

She opened her vision to see Irma's aura. A beautiful aqua with pale bands of silver shimmering around some of her joints.

"Ready?" Irma asked her.

Winnie dimmed her clairvoyant vision again. She suddenly felt nervous. What was she about to hear, see, and feel?

Would the fear and misery of some of these animals overwhelm Winnie once she passed through the reception door?

Irma clasped Winnie's right arm. It was a friendly and steadying gesture. Then the two of them stepped back into the belly of the shelter.

3

The main square footage of the expansive building was divided into different areas with their own separate hallways. Rows of kennels lined the hallway on the right and left. Winnie walked through that first gauntlet with Irma still clasping her arm.

"We'll start with the dogs," Irma said. "These are just some of them."

"How many animals do you have in all?" Winnie asked.

"A little over three hundred."

Winnie's heart gave a nervous jump. This was Tuesday. The Valentine Adopt-a-thon started on Friday.

How on earth was she going to get to all of them by then?

"Most of them are dogs," Irma said, "but about a third

are cats. And we have some parrots and other birds. We'll get to them last."

Winnie nodded, still feeling slightly stunned. Irma seemed to sense her hesitation.

"Oh, and I wanted to make sure you know that you'll get your money at the end of the week. It's just sitting in our account with the rest of Penny Bristol's donation."

Winnie had sent Irma her fee schedule the day before. Winnie's experience in Consumer Psychology taught her long ago that people only value what they pay for. She charged lawyer-like prices for her consultation work, knowing it would help her clients trust and follow her advice.

But this was the first time she would be billing against a retainer fund, just like a lawyer.

A few days' work would barely dent the twenty thousand dollars in that retainer. But Winnie was glad to know the money was already there, and that it would in no way deplete what Mrs. Bristol had already generously left for the Center.

And, Winnie reminded herself, in a way she, too, was a gift to the Center. She was here to help them sort out any of the animals' behavioral problems so that as many of them as possible could be adopted over the upcoming weekend.

"Ready?" Irma asked as they stood at the head of the two rows of kennels.

Winnie nodded. At least this should be interesting. Other than yesterday's brief experiment with Clover, she had never deliberately tried to communicate with animals before.

She began by opening her heart. By sending out love to the dogs she was about to meet.

My name is Winnie, she told them. *I am here to help you. Please tell me what I can do for you to make your lives better.*

A rush of sound boomed into Winnie's ears. The dogs were barking, some of them whining their high-pitched whines.

But the sounds weren't only outside her body, they were inside her mind, crowding to get her attention.

Winnie covered her ears with her hands. Then she shut down her internal hearing, the way she had trained herself to stop seeing the auras of everyone around her in a crowd. It was a form of self-preservation. Too much sensory stimulation would quickly exhaust her body and mind.

"Are you all right?" Irma asked her.

Winnie answered with a wry smile. "Just a little mistake," she confessed. Then she said out loud to the dogs in the room, "One at a time will be much easier. I promise I'll get to all of you."

Irma raised her eyebrows. But she let Winnie continue without asking any distracting questions.

They began walking slowly past each of the kennels.

Dogs rushed to the fronts of their wire cages, some of them barking, some wagging, some whimpering.

The sound of their voices echoed off the concrete walls and floor. But Winnie did her best to ignore the physical noise and to concentrate instead on the images and phrases streaming into her mind.

Some clairvoyants received information as though complete knowledge packets had been downloaded into their minds. Some relied on reading emotions. A few even received smells.

Winnie had always seen flashes of images that told her what she needed to know. She was also an auditory clairvoyant who heard words and phrases, spoken in her own voice inside her mind.

One of the continuing series of experiments at Amanda Birkauer's lab was to identify all the ways those with psi gifts received their knowledge of events past, present, and future.

Winnie paid close attention now to how she communicated with these animals. She would report all of it to Amanda later.

Hello, she told the dogs as she walked slowly past each kennel on the left and right. *I see you. Hello!* She silently greeted each of them as if they were coming up to her at a dog park.

But there were so many of them. Winnie was still

having difficulty separating the individuals from just the mass of striving energies within that room.

Although most of the dogs stood at the fronts of their kennels waiting to be seen and greeted, Winnie noticed that a few of them stayed pressed against the back corners of their enclosures, either too afraid or too dejected to come to the front.

These were the ones who needed her most. But she couldn't rush them to try to open up. Winnie would have to take her time. Just meeting all the dogs in this one section of the Center might require the rest of the morning.

She didn't want to worry about how long it might take. So she addressed it openly with Irma. "I might not get to all of them before Friday, you know. But I'll come here every day this week and next week, and however long I need to."

Irma smiled with relief. "Good. Thank you. We'll do our best. I'm sure it will be fine."

As Winnie continued walking slowly between the two rows, a phrase popped into her mind.

No one wants me.

Because the phrase came to her in Winnie's own voice, she didn't know which dog had sent it. She looked at the nearest dogs' faces, hoping to feel some connection.

One of them, a large white dog with a thick, fluffy coat and huge paws, stood at the front of his kennel wagging his tail. He met Winnie's gaze and panted in happy greeting. He was too joyful to have sent her that message.

She scanned the other kennels, but none of the other dogs seemed to reach out. Winnie gave up trying so hard to hear, and went back to slowly walking between the two rows.

When she and Irma reached the end of the long hall, Winnie stood against a closed door and surveyed the room.

Irma's staff kept the place clean. The shiny concrete floor looked like it was frequently mopped. The insides of the kennels looked free of any puddles of urine or piles of waste. Fresh bowls of water had been set out for all of the dogs. They each had a towel where they could curl up to find some warmth and a little cushioning from the hard concrete floor. Winnie suspected this was as nice of a shelter as any.

But as orderly as it was, as clean as Irma and her staff kept it, no amount of soap or bleach could hide what Winnie smelled.

It was a pungent, grimy odor that made her want to cover her nose with her hand. A smell of anguish. That was the only way she could think of it.

To be cooped up in these kennels, day after day, night after night—how would these poor dogs interpret what had happened?

Maybe some of them used to live in houses with soft

rugs or beds to lie on. Maybe some of them spent every day in a dusty back yard, or even tied to a stake with a chain.

Maybe some of them had never lived with humans, but had grown up fending for themselves as strays.

Winnie closed her eyes. Did she really want to know?

But Penny Bristol had asked her to do this. Penny Bristol wanted Winnie to help.

"Okay," Winnie said, more to herself than to Irma. "Let's go again. Kennel by kennel."

And this time, she could see them more clearly, dog by dog. They weren't just a mass of unfortunate animals all crowded in together.

Winnie cleared her mind. She told her sharpened senses this was all right. She remembered why she was here and what she hoped to do.

"Do you want to write this down?" Winnie asked.

Irma scrambled out through the closed door and quickly returned with a notepad and pen.

And finally Winnie could feel her mind settle in. She stopped blocking the information that wanted to come to her. Suddenly the images and words came flooding into her head. She realized she knew more about these animals than she believed she could when she first entered the room.

"Felix," Winnie said, pointing to the shepherd mix on

her right. "Likes cats, especially gray ones. There was one like that in the house where he was raised.

"Precious," she said, pointing to the middle-aged chihuahua shivering at the back of her kennel. "Kicked by the father of the family. Broken leg that they never took her to the vet for. She needs someone kind who just wants to love her and baby her."

"Are you sure?" Irma asked, lifting her pen from the notepad. She pointed to the index card fastened to the front of the kennel. "Says her name is Tinker. Some woman dropped her off."

"Huh," Winnie said, looking at the card. She shrugged. "I think she wants to be called Precious. Can you change the name?"

Irma smiled and wrote it down. "You bet." Then she knelt down in front of the chihuahua's kennel and made a kissing noise. "Precious?"

The little dog lifted her head. Winnie saw her two white ears spike at the sound of the name. The dog's big round eyes looked from Irma over to Winnie.

"Precious it is," Irma said with a smile.

Winnie couldn't be certain, but she thought the dog might be shivering a little less.

"This boy," Winnie said, approaching the fluffy white dog. "Guppy."

"Guppy?" Irma shook her head with a smile and wrote it down.

Winnie saw the name on the index card: Wolfy.

Nope, Guppy was a far more fitting name.

"Why is he here?" Winnie asked Irma.

"Stray. Found out in the desert. Don't let that thick coat fool you. It was a matted mess, and this guy was practically starving."

"How long has he been here?"

Irma consulted the index card. "A few weeks."

"Someone will take him this weekend," Winnie said. "I promise."

The dog gave a short bark and turned a circle in his kennel.

"Do you think he understood you?" Irma asked.

"I think he did," Winnie said.

Then she came to a kennel with a dog cowering in the corner. She looked bony. Her thin brown coat was bare in a few places. She kept her nose tucked down against her chest. She seemed to be trying to make herself as small as possible.

Winnie saw a boot. A fist. A rope yanked around the dog's neck.

She quickly shut off the image stream. She couldn't bear it.

"This one needs another dog in the family to show her how to be. She's had a very hard time. She needs a lot of patience and love."

Irma read the index card. She pointed to the given

name. Winnie shook her head.

"Lolly," she said, because the name popped into her mind. Irma wrote it down.

Before coming here, Winnie wouldn't have thought she should rename any of the dogs. But now for some of them it seemed exactly right.

Why should they start their new lives with kinder, better owners, and still have to respond to the names given them by their previous, unworthy humans?

Even the dogs like Guppy, formerly Wolfy, who had gotten their names from some well-meaning staff person at the Center, should be allowed to start fresh with whatever name Winnie could sense suited them better.

And maybe some of the animals wanted to name themselves. Like the chihuahua who wanted to be called Precious.

Winnie continued her slow return down the rows of kennels, and then she heard the phrase again.

No one wants me.

She paused in front of the wire enclosure where a blocky-headed tan dog lay with his nose on top of his paws. He looked like a pit bull mix of some sort. Maybe even part Lab, by the look of his thick tail.

Winnie waited for him to make eye contact, but he stared listlessly at his kennel wall.

"Hit by a car," Irma said. "At least the driver took him to an emergency vet and even paid for it. But then he didn't know what else to do. No tag, no microchip. So he brought him here."

Winnie looked at the name some staff person had given him. *Charlie.* That sounded all right to her.

"Char-lie," Winnie called in a soft, sing-song voice. The dog continued to lie motionless on the bare concrete. His towel lay crumpled in a corner.

What do you need? she asked him inside her mind.

No one wants me, he said again.

Winnie crouched in front of the kennel and curled her fingers around the wire.

Charlie, look at me. Why would you say that?

He shifted his eyes in her direction. But his chin still lay on his paws.

Winnie wasn't sure what else to do. This wasn't her specialty. What would Chandra, the pet communicator, do in her place?

Do you like the name Charlie? Someone here thought it was a good name for you. But you can choose any name you want.

Again the dog's eyes shifted to Winnie. Then he stared again at his kennel wall.

The door at the end of the hallway opened. Four people entered, three women and one man, all of them carrying leashes. Two of the women looked middle-aged. One of the women and the man seemed to be in their late twenties.

"Walkies!" the man called out, and the barking rose to an excited pitch. Winnie covered her ears with her hands.

"These are some of our volunteers," Irma told her as she turned aside to make room for them to pass.

Winnie gave them a quick glance, but then returned her attention to Charlie.

As the commotion rose around them, Charlie remained silent, but slightly lifted his head. One of his eyebrows creased upward into his smooth forehead. He warily watched the volunteers.

"Should we go to the next room?" Irma shouted over the excited barks.

It sounded reasonable, yet some instinct told Winnie to wait.

Her legs were cramping, but she remained crouched in front of Charlie's kennel. She continued to study the dog's behavior.

The two older women had already latched their leashes to two of the dogs and escorted them out of the room.

"They all get taken out to the exercise area twice a day," Irma said. "We're so lucky with our volunteers."

The younger woman smiled and gave Irma a little curtsy.

She was dressed like the other dog walkers, in jeans and an Animal Adoption Center T-shirt. She had curly black hair she wore back in a ponytail.

Charlie didn't like her. Winnie could feel it coming off him in waves. He wasn't afraid of her, but he didn't want her near.

The woman said, "Excuse me," and made a move toward opening Charlie's kennel.

Winnie creaked herself to standing and held out her hand for the leash.

"I'd like to walk him," Winnie said.

The young woman seemed surprised. She looked to Irma for direction.

"I don't think that's a good idea," the young woman said.

"It's all right, Crystal. Would you go get another leash? You can take out one of the others instead."

Crystal hesitated, but then she handed Winnie the leash. She smiled as though it wasn't a problem.

But Winnie could feel the woman's tension. She could see it in her eyes.

"Be careful," Crystal told her. "He's kind of a ... jerk."

Winnie could tell that Crystal wanted to call Charlie something else, but had modified it for the white-haired lady's benefit.

"He seems sweet to me," Winnie said.

Crystal shrugged. "He's gonna be hard to place. Just saying."

"Please don't say that in front of the dogs," Winnie

snapped. She was surprised at the strength of her reac-tion, but she could feel her blood pressure start to rise.

Crystal wrinkled her eyebrows. She looked to Irma.

"She's right," Irma said in a friendly enough voice. "Now go ahead and get another leash. You have dogs wait-ing. They'd love to be walked!"

As soon as Crystal left the room, Winnie and Irma were alone again with the dogs.

"We have a hard time keeping volunteers," Irma said. "This work can be … depressing."

"That one can go," Winnie told her. "She isn't good for the dogs. Is she, Charlie?"

The dog had his head up now and was looking at Winnie.

"Do you really think they can understand?" Irma asked. "I mean, I know what Mrs. Bristol said about you, but…" She twisted her rough hands together at her waist. "Tell me the truth. Because if I need to retrain everyone…"

"I think it's like surgery," Winnie said. "For years doctors and nurses said whatever they wanted about their patients during operations. They thought the patients couldn't hear them while they were under anesthetic.

"But then enough patients started reporting what they heard the surgeons say. They got it right, word for word. Now it's just accepted that everyone in the operating room should be careful what they say. Patients hear and they remember."

Irma thought about it. The door opened again and the male volunteer came for the next dog in line.

"Thanks, Chad," Irma told him. He smiled and continued his work.

As soon as they were alone again, Irma said, "You know, I've been worried about Charlie. After he came here, we kept him in the sick bay for several weeks until his leg healed. It's not that different from here—lots of dogs and cats in rows of kennels. But he always seemed so happy—even goofy. It's just that, ever since we brought him in here, he's seemed so depressed. I thought it was because he was missing his friends back in sick bay, but..."

"Does Crystal volunteer in the sick bay?"

"No. In fact, she just started a few weeks ago."

Winnie gave her a significant look.

"Okay, I understand. Either retraining, or she has to go."

A different kind of thought popped into Winnie's mind. "You have money now. Can't you hire more staff?"

"We're trying to build on to this place," Irma said. "Give all the animals more room. Penny did leave us a lot of money, but it still only goes so far. At some point the executor of her estate will sell her house, too, and then we'll get more then. But I wouldn't want to hurry little King Arthur along. Such a sweet dog."

Winnie felt an unexpected pain in the center of her chest.

She pressed her hand there, then tried to rub the pain away.

"Are you all right?" Irma asked.

"Hm." Winnie nodded, but she couldn't dismiss the stab she had just felt in her heart.

She wasn't worried about her health. She wasn't having a heart attack. She had felt pains like this before. Someone was trying to get her attention.

She looked into Charlie's kennel. He was sitting up on his haunches now and watching Winnie.

Had the pain come from him?

I'll take care of you, Charlie, Winnie told him with her mind.

The dog tilted his big blocky head and gave her a slight wag of his tail.

We'll find you a good home. Someone does want you. They just haven't met you yet. You're a sweet and lovely boy. Someone will be lucky to have you.

The dog groaned the way Clover sometimes did, in a way Winnie interpreted as a deep sigh. Charlie seemed to relax as he laid his chin back down on his paws.

One room, and already a few dogs Winnie felt she could help. First by renaming Precious, Guppy, and Lolly, and second by making sure Crystal didn't work with Charlie anymore.

She would do what she could with as many animals as possible before the weekend, but right now she felt especially committed to finding the right match for Charlie. It had to be someone who would love and appreciate this sensitive boy.

Winnie glanced at her watch. It was past noon.

If all the rooms were going to be like this one, she needed to eat and keep up her strength.

And then came that pain again just to the right of her heart.

She laid her hand flat over it.

Was one of the other animals calling to her right now, begging her to come and help?

She had been right to understand how daunting this experience would be.

But she had the skills to help in ways no one else here did.

And then she saw the image flash into her mind.

Suddenly Winnie knew exactly who was reaching out.

4

February days were short. It was already dusk by the time Winnie left the Animal Adoption Center.

She was bushed. Her mind felt fatigued. Her legs felt cramped from all the hours crouching in front of the kennels of dogs who needed her special attention.

Clover needed her dinner. Winnie needed hers, too.

And she needed to spend some time strategizing. Because there was another piece of work that was obviously hers to do.

Clover greeted her at the door, leading with her nose.

"Oh, I know. Where have I been?" Winnie said. "Who are all these dogs?"

She let Clover sniff her pants as thoroughly as she wanted.

But the dog would have to follow her around the

kitchen while she did it. Winnie needed bread. Two thick slices of the loaf she made yesterday, toasted. A bowl of leftover Hungarian mushroom soup. A whole bottle of fizzy water.

Clover finally gave up interest in Winnie's pants, in exchange for a full bowl of turkey-flavored kibble.

While her soup was reheating, Winnie sat on the couch and replenished her strength the best way she knew how, with an immediate dose of homemade chocolate chip cookies she kept on hand for emergencies just like this.

As the sugar rushed into her blood stream, Winnie closed her eyes and leaned her head back onto the cushions.

This might be tricky. Liars lied to the very end.

Clover finished inhaling her dinner and jumped up to join Winnie on the couch.

"What a day," Winnie told her. "But you know what? Your secret is out. I know you can talk to me now."

Clover opened her mouth and panted. Her tongue hung out comfortably between her teeth.

"I met some of the saddest dogs I've ever seen," Winnie said. Clover thumped her tail. "But we'll find them families. Even if it takes months. So I might not be home as much as usual for a while."

If Clover understood, Winnie couldn't tell from the way she was behaving. The dog stood up on the couch, turned around once in a circle, and then lay back down closer to Winnie. Winnie patted the Lab's rump and ate another cookie.

After her warm and filling dinner of soup and buttered toast, Winnie felt renewed enough to pick up her cell phone and make a call.

"I need some legal advice," she told her lawyer niece Rose. Then Winnie explained the image she had seen while she stood inside the room of kennels at the Center.

"Be careful," Rose said. "Do you want me to come with you?"

"Irma will come," Winnie said. "I'll call you as soon as we're done."

She disconnected the call and sat inside her warm and cozy house. Clover snored beside her. Winnie knew that both she and the dog led a very good life.

But not all dogs had that same privilege. And while Winnie couldn't help all of the dogs in the world, she could at least help a few.

And right now, she needed a plan to help one little dog in particular.

She had a few ideas about how to rescue Mrs. Bristol's dog, King Arthur.

Winnie closed her eyes and spoke to him. She hoped that he could hear her.

I'm coming, King Arthur. I heard you today. I'll come save you as soon as I can.

5

Wednesday, Winnie's second day at the Animal Adoption Center, and just two days away from the Valentine's Weekend Adopt-a-thon.

Irma introduced Winnie to one of her wizards in the back offices.

"This is Nessa." A woman in her early thirties smiled over at Winnie from where she sat behind a computer. She had light brown hair pulled back into a ponytail. She wore one of the Center's sweatshirts, this one in light gray. Winnie could see the woman's bloodshot blue eyes looking out at her from behind her large round glasses.

"How long have you been here?" Irma asked her.

Nessa glanced at the clock. "Since seven. But I got another thirty pictures entered." She made a fist into the air and croaked, "Woo-hoo!"

"Nessa writes up all the animal profiles for our website," Irma explained. "We got a little behind."

Nessa was back to typing. "*I* got a little behind," she said good-naturedly without looking up.

"A newborn will do that," Irma said. "Who's watching her?"

"My mom today, Dave tomorrow. He's taking off work so I can get this all done."

"Well, we won't keep you," Winnie said. She could feel the tension streaming off of the woman's shoulders.

"Hey," Nessa said as Winnie and Irma made for the door. "I like all the new names. They really suit them. I think some of them even look happier in their photos now."

Winnie hated to bother her, but now she was too curious to let it go. "Do you have Charlie yet?"

Nessa clicked a few keys and motioned for Winnie to come read the screen over her shoulder.

This was not the face Winnie had seen yesterday. "When did you take this?" she asked.

Irma looked, too. "In the sick bay about a month ago."

No wonder Irma had been worried about the change in his disposition. Charlie had gone from a wide, toothy grin to the somber dog Winnie saw in his kennel yesterday.

"Here's his buddy," Nessa said, clicking over to a different profile. Winnie saw an orange tabby kitten, overloaded with cuteness, reaching out her paws and staring with her big eyes into the camera.

"I'm hoping someone will take them together," Nessa said. "Wouldn't that be sweet? I think all the kittens in that litter have been cleared now for adoption."

"We don't require it, of course," Irma told Winnie, "but sometimes people are willing to take bonded pairs."

"That's always our favorite," Nessa said.

Winnie could understand why.

Two animals rescued in one adoption. She had a new focus for her work today.

She would ask the animals she spoke to whether they had a friend they hoped could go to the same home with them.

Winnie checked her watch. "We should get started."

This was going to be a somewhat shortened day.

Winnie had already made a few phone calls from the parking lot of the Center just after nine o'clock. The people she spoke to confirmed what she suspected.

So she made one more phone call, arranging for an appointment this afternoon.

Piece by piece, Winnie's plan was shifting into place within her mind.

But first she had animals to help here at the Center. Irma grabbed her notebook from the day before and found another pen, then she and Winnie stepped into one of the cat rooms.

Good morning! I'm Winnie. I'm here to help you all find good homes. Please tell me what kinds of things you like and don't like. Tell me if you have any special friends here. Then we'll try to match you with the perfect person.

The din was different from a roomful of barking dogs. The cats sounded more like a burbling stream compared to a roaring waterfall.

Winnie smiled inside her heart. She loved to use her gifts this way.

The kennels were stacked three high and then side by side to fill out the two rows. Winnie looked at the nametag on the first kennel: Scat.

He was an older black cat with a little divot taken out of his right ear. There were white patches on his front paws. The cat looked at Winnie with wide and curious yellow eyes. She poked her finger through the wires and Scat licked it with the delicate tip of his tongue.

The information popped into Winnie's mind. Suddenly she knew something about this cat.

"He hates that name," Winnie told Irma. "His last owner gave it to him." Irma raised her pen to her pad. Winnie listened for a moment for a new name to pop just as easily into her head.

Instead Winnie saw an image of the black cat sleeping on top of a white upholstered chair. Sunlight streamed in through a window and warmed his silky back.

A kind-looking middle-aged woman sat on a chair

beside him, reading a book. She reached over to stroke the cat's head. Winnie could feel how much he loved the woman's touch.

Winnie sensed this wasn't a scene from Scat's past. The cat inside the kennel looked too skinny and bedraggled to have come from a pampered life like that.

But as soon as she stopped trying to analyze the image, and allowed herself simply to feel the emotions of the cat instead, Winnie understood. She looked into Scat's eyes and smiled.

The black cat had obviously listened to what Winnie said when she first entered the room. *Tell me what kinds of things you like and don't like.*

The black cat was sending Winnie a wish.

She kept her index finger curled around the wire of his cage. He licked her knuckle again.

"You need a better name," she told him. "Something fun and sweet to go with your new life. And maybe something ... a little sassy." The name sprang into Winnie's mind. "Boots." Because of his white paws. But then she heard the rest of it: "Boots McCoy."

It was the first time she had given any of the animals a surname. Boots McCoy seemed to approve. He answered with a loud and hearty meow.

Irma laughed and wrote down the new name.

Winnie could have spent the next hour talking with

the cat, but she had to move on to all the others. Time was ticking away.

And King Arthur was very much on her mind.

Winnie sometimes thought of her clairvoyant ability as a flashlight she held inside a dark and vast warehouse. She couldn't just flip on a light and see everything at once. Instead her clairvoyance showed her whatever was focused within the limited beam.

Sometimes reading a word or a name made information suddenly pop into her mind. The same if she saw a photograph. She would receive information about that person or thing or place.

Standing in a room of dog kennels yesterday, Winnie had asked Irma if the Center could use some of Mrs. Bristol's bequest to hire more people for the staff.

"Penny did leave us a lot of money, but it still only goes so far. At some point the executor of her estate will sell her house, too, and then we'll get more then. But I wouldn't want to hurry little King Arthur along. Such a sweet dog."

Then Winnie had felt a pain in her chest.

Because hearing the name King Arthur had clicked on her flashlight.

The beam of light swung around and located the little dog.

And what Winnie saw of him made her heart hurt.

Five or six years ago, when Winnie saw him riding on top of a little blue blanket on top of Penny Bristol's rolling walker, King Arthur was a handsome, well-groomed dog who, even though he was in pain from his misplaced rib, still looked healthy and well-fed.

In the image that flashed into Winnie's mind yesterday, King Arthur now looked skinny and sick, with goopy discharge coming from his eyes. He took long, wheezy breaths as though something were wrong with his lungs.

His coat looked dirty and matted. Obviously he wasn't being groomed every week by Pierre LeFranc, as specified within Mrs. Bristol's will.

That had been one of Winnie's calls this morning. Mr. LeFranc confirmed in an icy tone that he had been informed that his services were no longer required.

"Who fired you?" Winnie asked him.

"That Charlotte woman," he said.

Charlotte Amper, the dog's caretaker designated in Mrs. Bristol's will.

A second call confirmed that Margery, the cook who made all of the spaniel's favorite foods, had also been fired within the first week after Charlotte Amper took over the house.

"I don't know why," Margery said. "It's dumb. I was fully paid for. She could have had me cook for her the whole time she was there."

Winnie suspected the reason. "What happened to your salary once you left?"

"I assume it went back into the household expense

account," said Margery. "Not that she needed it. Do you know how much was already there?"

She told Winnie the figure. It was even more than she had imagined.

"Why so much?" Winnie asked.

"Because Mrs. Bristol grew up poor," Margery said. "She told me how happy it made her never to have to worry anymore whether she could afford groceries or gas or anything else that was so hard for her parents to buy. She didn't even mind going to the dentist, because her father told her only rich people could afford good teeth."

Winnie admired Mrs. Bristol even more for leaving most of her wealth to a charity that took care of animals.

Last night, Winnie's niece Rose confirmed that if someone wasn't abiding by the terms of a will, the executor of the estate could remove their right to receive anything further.

And if someone defrauded the estate by taking money and goods that weren't theirs to have, then the estate could sue, and there might even be criminal liability for theft.

But Winnie hoped it wouldn't come to that.

She had a different plan in mind.

At noon she ate the peanut butter and strawberry jam sandwich she had packed for herself this morning. Then she and Irma continued visiting as many of the animals as they could before Winnie's watch alarm reminded her it was time to leave.

"We might not be back before close," Irma told the purple-haired receptionist, Kirsten.

Irma had changed into a clean Animal Adoption Center sweatshirt, and had given Winnie one to wear, too.

They drove in Irma's dusty, dinged-up Toyota 4Runner, since it had the Center's logo on the side.

Winnie wanted to look as official as possible.

Irma drove north for forty minutes, eventually coming to the wealthy subdivisions in the Catalina foothills. She had been to Penny Bristol's house before. She described it to Winnie on the way.

Mrs. Bristol's husband, Robert, had earned his fortune from inventing some manufacturing process Irma didn't know much about. He and Penny had traveled all around the world and had collected exotic furniture and art from the places where they went.

"Their house is like a museum," Irma said. "Very beautiful and tasteful. I could tell Penny was really proud of the things she and Robert collected."

As they pulled into the paved driveway in front of the large and elegant two-story house, Winnie said, "It's better if we don't say too much. Silence makes people nervous. They want to talk just to fill in the gaps. So we'll tell her why we're here, and then wait for her to explain."

Winnie checked her watch again. It was a little before

four o'clock. Her appointment was in a half hour. She hoped she would be ready by then.

Irma rang the doorbell. Winnie could hear its musical notes chiming inside the house.

When a few minutes passed without any answer, Irma rang the bell again.

Winnie looked around at the front of the property. She remembered the will providing for landscaping, but most of the plants looked blackened from freezing, and only the various cacti had survived.

At last they heard some movement from inside the house.

Winnie reached over and pressed the doorbell again. She wanted to make sure Charlotte Amper felt properly annoyed.

"I'm coming!" a voice shouted.

Winnie smiled at Irma and pressed the doorbell again.

The door opened and Winnie had to adjust her line of sight by about half a foot lower than it was.

She expected to see someone her own height, but Charlotte Amper couldn't have been taller than five feet.

She added at least four more inches to her stature by wearing a tall, ratty wig with coils of black hair stacked on top of each other the way women in the 1800s might have worn it.

She looked like she might be in her late fifties, but the years had taken their toll. Her skin had a yellowish tint.

Her eyes were only half open. Winnie could smell cigarette smoke on her wig and skin and clothes. And Charlotte Amper's breath reeked of alcohol.

She wore faded red sweatpants, bedroom slippers, and a T-shirt celebrating a steak house.

"Who are you?" Charlotte asked them.

"Remember me?" Irma asked, smiling. "I'm Irma Makelski from the Animal Adoption Center, and this is Dr. Parsons."

Winnie had told Irma to use her formal designation of doctor. It made a useful impression in a situation like this.

"Doctor?" Charlotte repeated.

"Yes," Winnie said. "We're here from the Center. Mrs. Bristol instructed us to make home visits every quarter."

Charlotte's eyes widened. She cursed under her breath.

"Hold on, hold on…" And she started closing the door.

"Oh no, Ms. Amper," Winnie said, pushing it back open. "Our instructions are to show up unannounced and see the condition of the house and Mrs. Bristol's dog exactly as they are."

Charlotte Amper's bottom lip sucked in and out while Winnie could see her brain frantically working.

She almost felt sorry for the woman, but the image of King Arthur still burned in her mind.

"Where is the dog?" Winnie asked.

Charlotte stared at her with wide open amber eyes.

Winnie waited. She took her own advice and did not try to fill the uncomfortable silence with words.

It took several long moments before Charlotte Amper repeated, "The dog..." She glanced behind her as if King Arthur might be right there underfoot.

Winnie surveyed the part of the room visible from the door. It did not look like a museum, the way Irma had described it. It looked like a frat house after a party.

There were bottles and cans and plates crusted with old food. The house smelled of cigarettes and garbage.

Charlotte Amper was a pig.

Winnie could see Irma scanning the room, too. It must be worse for her, having seen it in its former glory.

"Wasn't there a painting over there?" Irma asked, pointing.

Charlotte turned around and stayed in that position longer than seemed necessary.

"Yeah..." she finally said, and then she left it at that.

"The *dog*," Winnie said, more forcefully this time. This wasn't a game. She wasn't amused. King Arthur was somewhere in this house, suffering.

"I'll get him," Charlotte said, and she made some slight movement toward her left.

But Winnie suddenly felt a rising panic. She needed to see the dog *now*.

"Take us to him. This instant," Winnie said. She

pushed into the house and glared at the woman who had so abused Penny Bristol's trust.

Charlotte looked from Winnie to Irma, as though trying to think of some angle that still might work, but then her shoulders sagged. She must have realized she was well and truly caught.

She led the two of them through what had once been a beautiful living room, then into the kitchen where the garbage was piled up even worse than Winnie expected.

She almost asked, "What is *wrong* with you?" But she knew what was wrong. She had studied psychology for enough years that she knew a disturbed mind when she saw it.

Again, she might have felt sorry for Charlotte Amper if the woman simply kept her destruction to herself. But she had preyed on Mrs. Bristol, promising her she would take care of King Arthur and this home.

Winnie hated liars. And she could never forgive anyone who would hurt a dog.

Charlotte continued leading them toward a door at the back of the house.

She opened it onto a laundry room.

King Arthur looked up from his dirty dog bed on the floor.

The small room had no windows. At least the light was on.

Irma knelt on the tile and spoke softly to the dog. King Arthur whimpered in response.

Despite the impression she wanted to give, Dr. Parsons was not a veterinarian. She let Irma examine the dog. Winnie stood in the doorway, while Charlotte Amper waited nervously outside.

Irma began describing all that was wrong. "These nails haven't been cut for three months. I'm sure he can barely walk. He has some kind of infection in his eyes and ears. And it sounds like he might have pneumonia."

Winnie could hear his wheezing breath, just as she heard it the day before.

The dog looked at Irma through his gunky eyes. He whimpered at her touch.

Irma picked up his bed, with King Arthur cradled inside. Winnie stepped out of the room and Irma carried the dog past Charlotte Amper.

"I can't even speak to you, I'm so angry," she told Charlotte with venom in her eyes.

And true to her word, Irma continued carrying the dog through the house and out the front door, presumably to settle him gently in the backseat of her car.

The doorbell rang, and Winnie knew it wasn't Irma.

She checked her watch. Right on time. She strode to the front door to receive her guest.

The young man wore blue cotton workpants and a shirt with his name over the pocket.

"Hello, Kyle," Winnie said. "I don't know how many doors there are. Go ahead and do whatever you need."

His van was parked in the driveway behind Irma's Toyota. The sign on the side said *A-Best Mobile Locksmith*.

"What's he here for?" Charlotte Amper demanded.

"He's changing the locks. You're moving out right now."

Charlotte's bottom lip sputtered in and out again. She grabbed her lofty wig and threw it to the ground. Her unhealthy habits had left her with gray, gristly hair. Although even that looked better than the wig.

"You can't do this!" Charlotte shouted, but Winnie calmly stared her down.

"Fraud is a crime. We've spoken to the estate's lawyer. You have bigger worries than where you're going to stay tonight."

Charlotte looked frantically around the living room. She reminded Winnie of someone realizing her house was on fire, and trying to decide in a split second what to save.

"Do you have clothes?" Winnie asked.

"'Course I have clothes!"

"Then let's go pack them. You only have an hour."

Irma came back into the house at a trot. She deliberately refused to look at Charlotte.

"I need to get him to the vet," Irma said. "I'm sure I'll

have to leave him overnight. I'll come back and get you as soon as I can."

"Or I can call a taxi," Winnie said. "Don't worry about me. Please just make sure little Arthur is all right."

Then she felt a tug on her heart. She couldn't just let the dog leave. Winnie ran out after Irma.

King Arthur lay on his dirty bed in the backseat, wheezing with every breath.

Winnie stroked the dog's head. She leaned over and spoke to him softly.

"Thank you for telling me. You saved yourself. We'll take good care of you now, I promise."

She kissed his soft brown head between his long warm ears. Warm with an infection. Winnie recognized the smell of it from the few bouts of ear infection Clover had over the years.

But this one smelled much worse. She hoped the dog wouldn't lose his hearing as a result.

Winnie stroked her thumb across the little dog's forehead. Then she said goodbye and shut the door and let Irma drive him away.

Kyle the locksmith was still working on the front door. He had finished the knob and already moved on to the deadbolt.

Winnie drew in a breath of fresh air before plunging back into the filthy house. She knew by the time she got home tonight, her hair and clothes would smell of cigarettes.

She found Charlotte Amper upstairs in the master bedroom, messily throwing her clothes into a duffel bag.

For a moment Winnie considered searching the bag to make sure Charlotte hadn't stolen anything from the room.

There might be expensive jewelry in there. And probably mementos that had meant something to Mrs. Bristol.

But Charlotte had had total freedom inside this house for the past three months. Maybe she had already sold the painting in the living room that Irma thought was missing. She might have already stolen and sold Mrs. Bristol's jewelry, too. And who knew how many other items she might have taken that Mrs. Bristol trusted her to leave to be sold at some future time, with the proceeds all going to the Animal Adoption Center.

Winnie couldn't understand how a woman like Charlotte Amper ever gained Mrs. Bristol's trust. But like all con people, Charlotte must have put on a convincing act.

She probably dressed better and made sure she didn't stink of alcohol. She probably coddled the little dog, spoke baby talk to him—who knew. Mrs. Bristol must have seen something she liked in Charlotte Amper.

Winnie felt nothing but contempt for the con woman.

At times like these, Winnie had to fight some deep-seated urge to scold and lecture and to try to shame.

If someone like Charlotte Amper felt any shame right now, it was only because she had gotten caught. Somewhere in the forming of her character, she had missed the self-regulating chip that told her to stop before ever hurting people this way.

"This is mine," Charlotte said defensively as she grabbed a frilly robe off of its hanger.

Winnie doubted it was true, but she didn't care at the moment. She just wanted the Amper woman gone.

Charlotte Amper shoved a few more shirts into her duffel, then she zipped it up and hauled it onto her stooped shoulder.

Winnie followed her down the stairs. Charlotte cast her gaze around the bottom floor. But with Winnie tailing her so closely, she must have decided that any further theft wasn't worth it.

She bullied her way past burly young Kyle, and she headed toward the garage.

Winnie continued following her. She was aware of the Cadillac that must be inside.

Charlotte looked back, no doubt to see if anyone was watching. She made a face at Winnie, then dug out a set of keys from the front pocket of her dirty, faded red sweatpants.

She punched in a code to the control pad at the side of the garage. The door quietly slid up, revealing the

Cadillac and an old beater Chevy Celebrity in the space beside it.

Charlotte opened the back door of the Celebrity and threw her duffel on the seat. Then she got in and fired up the rough-sounding engine.

The car sputtered and belched out smoke from the tailpipe. But it worked, and Charlotte put in reverse.

She left the garage door up. Winnie didn't know the code to put it down. She hoped it was written someplace for someone to find—

And there. The four numbers flashed into Winnie's mind. Her clairvoyant flashlight had found the keypad in that dark, vast warehouse.

Charlotte passed Winnie and made a rude gesture out of her window.

Winnie ignored her and went to close the garage door.

As she walked back to the house, Winnie started making a mental list of all the things she could do now to make everything better.

The estate had all the money it needed to hire cleaners and landscapers and appraisers and whatever else Mrs. Bristol's house and its contents might need.

But she came to a halt in front of Kyle's locksmith van, and realized she had no part to play anymore.

She was only a bystander in this twisted situation. This was for other people to fix.

Her work was back at the Animal Adoption Center

right now. There were so many animals there she still needed to meet.

Her car was still there, too. But it was getting late. She needed to get home to feed Clover.

Winnie called Irma's cell phone, but it went straight to voicemail. She must not have it on while she was at the vet.

Winnie left a message. "I'll take a cab home. Don't worry about me. And I'll take a cab to the Center in the morning. We'll just add it to my bill."

But then an image flashed into Winnie's mind.

She was sure Mrs. Bristol would approve.

"Actually," Winnie continued on Irma's voicemail, "I'll take Mrs. Bristol's car home. We can bring it back here tomorrow."

Winnie clicked off the call. She could see in her mind's eye exactly where the Cadillac keys were hanging on a hook inside the front door.

She found the keys, but now she was missing Kyle. She could hear him somewhere at the back of the house.

"I need to go," she told him. "Does someone have to be here while you work?"

"Nope, we're insured and I'm incredibly honest."

The young man grinned at Winnie, and she opened her vision to look at the young man's aura.

"Yes, I believe you are," she told him. She fished out her slim wallet from the pocket of her navy blue vest and pulled out two twenty dollar bills. Although the estate lawyer had told her that the estate would pay for the locksmith, Winnie wanted to tip him herself.

The Cadillac was relatively clean. Charlotte must not have driven it very much.

Winnie thought of the provision in Section 6 of Penny Bristol's will that would pay for gas so Charlotte Amper could drive King Arthur around to look at the foothills scenery.

That poor little dog. Winnie could only hope he would be all right.

As for the liar and thief Charlotte Amper, Winnie would leave it to the estate's lawyer to decide what to do.

Winnie started up the Cadillac and checked the gas gauge. There was still half a tank. More than enough to get home.

The sun had already set by the time she arrived home. Once again Clover sniffed her clothes and gave Winnie a thorough inspection.

Winnie could smell the cigarette smoke on her clothes. She gave Clover her dinner, then undressed and took a long shower.

By the time she got out, there was a message on her phone. Irma had called with an update on King Arthur.

She had been right about the infections in his eyes and ears, and right that he had pneumonia.

The vet was keeping him overnight to give him antibiotics and liquids in an IV. The dog was seriously malnour-ished and dehydrated.

As Winnie listened to the list of ailments, she could feel her skin getting warmer as the anger inside her rose.

But she had learned long ago that anger did not moti-vate her, it only drained her. So she concentrated on letting the red rage subside.

Her gift had allowed her to hear King Arthur's plea. That was what mattered now. Winnie was grateful she could help a poor dog in need. That should be her focus.

But she spared a thought for where Charlotte Amper was now. And her mind provided the answer.

Winnie saw the woman in a dark, dingy house, smoking and drinking from a tall can of beer.

This must be where she lived when she met Penny Bristol. She had to have lived somewhere.

So now she would simply resume her former life.

And maybe look for the next person she could fool into thinking she was trustworthy and would take good care of their dog after the person was gone.

Winnie shook her head to clear it. She didn't want to know any more about that Amper woman.

Instead, she sent out a loving thought to King Arthur.

Sleep well, and I'll see you tomorrow.

As busy as she knew she would be at the Center, Winnie knew she would also need to see King Arthur. The little dog had wedged himself like a sliver inside

Winnie's heart. She needed to see him happy and well again.

It was probably too soon to think of him being placed with a loving family at the Valentine's Adopt-a-thon, but Winnie knew that Irma would find him a good home when it was time.

Winnie reheated some of the lasagna she had made over the weekend. Then she sat with Clover on the couch and reflected on the day.

The dog scooted closer to Winnie, then laid her head on Winnie's lap. It was exactly what Winnie needed.

Some night soon King Arthur would be sitting with someone just like this. Winnie could picture it in her mind. His eyes were clear, he had been bathed and brushed, and his ribs no longer showed through his coat.

A hand stroked softly down the little dog's side. He sighed and settled in closer.

There was another dog's nose sharing the person's lap from the other side.

How sweet. King Arthur would have a brother or sister.

But then the image shifted upward, and showed Winnie the whole room.

"No," she said, with a laugh of surprise. But it was too late to deny it, she had already seen this glimpse of the future.

Her visions didn't lie. But Winnie knew that the future

was never set. People had free will. The future was always malleable.

But did Winnie want to change this particular future? Now that she had seen how it could be?

Winnie sitting in the center of her couch, Clover on one side, sweet little King Arthur on the other.

Winnie still wasn't certain that she and Clover could communicate this way, but she experimented anyway by forwarding the image to Clover's mind.

"What do you think?" Winnie asked her out loud. "Do you want a little brother? Actually, he's probably older than you. But he is smaller."

Whether it was from the sound of Winnie's voice or because Clover actually knew what Winnie was saying, the Labrador thumped her tail.

"You should meet him first. See if you like him," Winnie said. Clover thumped her tail again.

She could resist this future, but why would she want to? Maybe Clover had been wishing she had a friend.

Winnie returned Irma's call. Irma sounded tired, but she seemed upbeat about King Arthur's recovery.

"I think I have a new home for him," Winnie said.

"You do? That's great!"

Winnie told her the happy news.

"It's too perfect," Irma said. "Do you know how happy Penny would be? She would love to know that you were taking care of her dog for the rest of his life."

Winnie could feel it, too. A comforting warmth inside her chest.

She had no doubt that Penny Bristol would approve.

Before Irma let her go, she wanted Winnie to give her all the nitty-gritty details about the eviction of Charlotte Amper.

Winnie found she could tell it now without feeling any rage.

Because although King Arthur had to endure three terrible months, in the end, everything had come out all right.

Irma yawned. "I'm beat. I want to be at the Center early tomorrow. See you in the morning."

"I'll be there," Winnie promised.

Then she sat on the couch with Clover and thought about Mrs. Bristol's little dog.

Winnie sometimes wondered if people understood the magic in their own lives.

The cause and effect. How their good deeds could lead to good in return.

And how despite the way it sometimes seemed in the short run, in the long run the universe seemed to tilt in favor of eventually letting the good guys win.

Penny Bristol was generous and kind. She left her wealth to help homeless animals.

She left a separate fund for the Animal Adoption Center to hire Winnie Parsons.

While Winnie was helping them, she saw a vision of King Arthur.

Some might say that Winnie and Irma saved Penny Bristol's dog. But it was really Mrs. Bristol's kindness and generosity that saved her dog.

Winnie could draw the step-by-step diagram in her mind. Irma was right, it was actually perfect.

And along that same path, Winnie had met the animals at the shelter. And she would continue working hard to help all of them find new homes.

"It's too much," Winnie told Clover. "Too much!" She kissed Clover's soft yellow head.

She had to put herself to bed so she could get up early, too. Tomorrow was Thursday. She had so many animals still to meet before the Adopt-a-thon on Friday.

But as she settled between her flannel sheets, and Clover hopped up to claim her spot at the foot of the bed, Winnie could picture the little spaniel who would fit nicely on her other side.

In the morning, Winnie drove the Cadillac to the Center. She rushed in ready to start the day.

"Come on," Irma told her, taking Winnie by the arm. "Nessa has something to tell you."

Nessa still looked tired, either because of her newborn or because she had already been at her computer for hours, or more probably both.

But she let out a yip when she saw Winnie standing in

her doorway. Nessa motioned excitedly for her to come look at the computer screen.

"Yesterday," Nessa said. "After you and Irma left." Then she leaned back in her chair and held out her hands to the screen like she was serving it to Winnie on a platter.

Charlie's photo was there, with his happy, grinning face. Next to it was the photo of an orange tabby kitten.

"Both of them," Nessa said. "Adopted together! A family with two kids came and took them right out of here."

"But how did they—" Winnie started to ask.

"They saw them on the website," Irma said. "Nessa's brilliant work."

Nessa blew on her fingernails and buffed them against her chest, a well-earned gesture of pride.

Winnie thought of the sad dog she had met just two days ago.

No one wants me.

She had promised him he would find his family, and that promise came true.

And to have his little kitten friend along. It was too sweet and wonderful for words.

"Okay, let's go," Winnie told Irma. Now that she had a taste of the thrill of seeing two of these animals adopted, she wanted to help get every single one of them find a new home.

She had refined her techniques over the past two days.

Her interviews flowed faster and more smoothly. By the end of Thursday afternoon, she had visited all of the dogs and cats.

There were still the birds, and a few ferrets, and an iguana, and other assorted pets. She would have to get to them on Monday.

Although the Valentine's Weekend Adopt-a-thon was the Center's big event, Charlie and his kitten friend had proven that people would look for pets on the website, too.

And more animals would keep coming in, because that was the nature of shelters. Winnie would still be needed, and she was happy to help.

But for now she just wanted to get back in her own car and drive to the vet's office before it closed.

King Arthur had responded well to the antibiotics and hydration. If Winnie wanted to, she could take him home tonight.

He would still need medication and extra care for a few more weeks, but the veterinarian thought the danger was over.

They had bathed him there, and clipped his overgrown toenails, and someone had brushed out his fur. He didn't look as dapper as he did when Winnie first met him, but at least he was clean again.

They brought him out to the lobby, and she bent down and scooped King Arthur into her arms.

"Do you want to come home with me?" Winnie asked him.

The dog's eyes were clear now, not gooped with infection.

King Arthur looked into Winnie's eyes and his tongue came out and he happily panted.

She was used to Clover's thick Labrador tail swishing against Winnie's leg or thumping on the furniture.

But King Arthur's smaller tail would do just as well, and it told Winnie everything she needed to know.

It wagged against her arm as the dog panted and lightly wheezed. Winnie could feel the dog's heart beating against his ribs.

One of those ribs had slipped out of place before, leading Penny Bristol to bring her dog—of all places—to the parapsychology lab.

Winnie had been the one to help her. And now here was Winnie again.

Holding the little spaniel in her arms. Hugging him close to her heart.

Penny Bristol was magic, and she never knew it.

But Winnie hoped that somehow Penny Bristol knew it now.

thank you for
loving dogs.

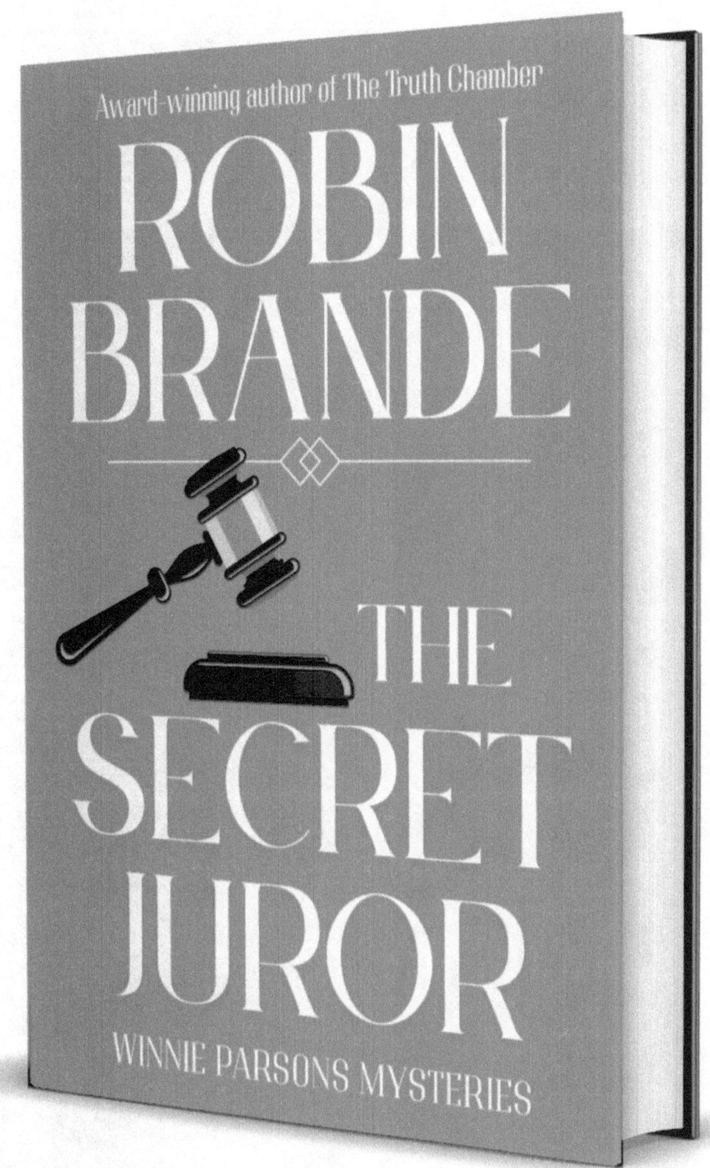

Liars can't hide
from Winnie Parsons.
But they sure keep trying.

The mind is a mysterious place. And the truth can change your life.

Heart-warming stories of love, courage, and compassion in a not-so-distant future

Stories of life after death, miracle healings, communication with other species, and more.

ABOUT THE AUTHOR

Robin Brande is an award-winning author, former trial attorney, black belt in martial arts, wilderness medic, and Reiki Master.

She writes in multiple genres, including mystery, fantasy, science fiction, young adult, romance, and self-help. She is also a designer and maker whose work celebrates the bookish life.

For more information:
robinbrande.com